The Seven Professors of the Far North

John Fardell works as a freelance cartoonist, illustrator, designer and occasional puppeteer. A regular contributor to *Viz* (he is the creator of 'The Modern Parents' and 'The Critics' amongst others), his work has also appeared in the *Independent*, the *List*, the *Herald*, the *New Statesman* and the *Evening Standard*. He is married with two boys and lives in Edinburgh.

The 7 Professors of the Far North

John Fardell

ff

faber and faber

First published in 2004
by Faber and Faber Limited
3 Queen Square London WC1N 3AU

Typeset by Faber and Faber Limited
Printed in England by Bookmarque Ltd, Croydon

A CIP record for this book
is available from the British Library

ISBN 0–571–22155–6

10 9 8 7 6 5 4

To Jenny,
Joshua & Connor,
with love

Prologue

'STOP HIM! KILL HIM!'

A lanky scarecrow of a man tore across the frozen ground, jinking this way and that as bullets blasted up snow and ice around him. *Cover . . . Get behind hut . . . Now where? . . . There — snowmobile! . . . Unguarded . . .* The man flung himself onto the large grey machine, gloved hands fumbling with the ignition.

PTANG! PTANG! Bullets on metal. *Come on . . Start!. . Come ON . . Yes! . . .*

The engine roared alive, powering the vehicle forward at breakneck speed. *More men . . . blocking way . . . raising their guns . . . Straight through 'em! . . .* Scattering the guards, the fugitive forced the machine on at full throttle, long coat flying out behind, battered hat and face muffler covering all but his eyes. Haunted eyes; desperate eyes; searching for a way down to the shore.

Rocks. Have to jump 'em.

He zoomed the snowmobile up a snowdrift, into an arcing leap over the snow-covered rocks. WHAM! The vehicle slammed onto the frozen sea, almost jolting the rider from his seat, and sped onwards.

PTANG! PTANG!.. PFUT! I'm hit! No - just a bullet grazing hat. Keep swerving. Are they following me? Bound to be. Keep eyes on ice ahead. Starting to snow again. Good - it'll cover tracks.

The swirling snow closed in, obliterating the horizon ahead and the island behind, enveloping the rider and his vehicle in a white void.

Set course: dead south. Any damage to machine? Seems alright. Fuel? Main tank full. Two spare cans; both look intact. Maybe I have a chance. A slim chance. Damn slim.

Nearly seven hundred miles of rugged, treacherous sea ice lay between him and the northern coast of Russia. *Air temperature: minus 55°C . . . Food rations: inadequate.* With the added danger of enemy snowmobiles and enemy planes, death seemed almost certain.

But I have to try . . . Have to alert the others . . . Tell them Murdo's secret . . . If I fail, it's the end of everything . . . The end for all humanity . . .

Chapter One

Eleven-year-old
Sam Carnabie
sat on the edge
of his bed and
finished packing his
favourite things into his small rucksack. Actually, the
rucksack itself was one of his favourite things. It was a
recent present from his dad. Not a Christmas or birthday
present either, but one of the I-saw-this-in-town-and-
thought-you-might-like-it presents with which his dad
occasionally surprised him. It was made of strong grey-blue
canvas and brown leather and looked tough enough for a
real expedition. Best of all, it had loads of compartments
and side pockets with chunky brass zips.

His ordinary stuff, such as clothes, toothbrush and comb,
fitted easily into the main bag, leaving the side pockets free
for his most prized possessions:

A Swiss army knife (with 14 different blades and tools,
including screwdrivers, pliers and a small hacksaw).

The binoculars he'd got for Christmas (really compact
but very powerful).

His combined-travel-alarm-clock-compass-and-
magnifying-glass (water resistant to a depth of 30 metres).

The torch he'd got for his last birthday (which could
be set to white, red or green, wide beam, narrow beam,
constant or flashing).

3

Sam sighed. What a waste – all this stuff perfectly packed, the first Saturday of the Easter holiday and he wasn't going on a real expedition at all, but for a week-long visit with his parents to his Great-Aunt Roberta's oppressively tidy house in Reading. Great-Aunt Roberta liked cats and china ornaments of cats but didn't much like children.

Well, it couldn't be helped. Sam's parents, both food scientists, had to be in Reading for the week to attend a conference (New Developments in Canned Vegetable Technology) and all the school friends with whom Sam might have stayed were away for the holidays themselves.

Remembering from previous visits that there wasn't even a proper park near the house, Sam slipped some pencils, pens and a well-used notebook into the back of the rucksack. The notebook was half-full of drawings he'd made of his inventions: a pedal-powered airship, a wind-driven cable-car system, that sort of thing. At least he'd have plenty of free time to draw some more.

The overcast weather did nothing to improve Sam's spirits as he put his rucksack onto the back seat of his parents' car. His mum had just brought the last suitcase out of the house and Sam was about to get into the car himself, when a bright yellow motorbike and sidecar swung round the corner and rumbled to a halt in front of them.

Sam stared at the vehicle. It looked out of place in their ordinary Hertfordshire suburb. The massive bike was festooned with metal tubes, lamps, dials and dozens of complicated gadgets, the functions of which Sam could barely begin to guess. The sidecar was long and torpedo shaped, topped by a Perspex canopy. It looked to Sam just as if someone had sliced the middle out of a small aero-plane and streamlined the ends. The whole magnificent miscellany of sunshine yellow and shimmering chrome radiated an enticing smell of engine oil and old leather which made Sam's tummy tingle inside.

The motorbike's rider, a gangly man wearing a blue greatcoat which had seen better days, gave a cheerful beep on the horn and waved to them. The sidecar's two passengers, a brown-faced boy and girl, also waved. Sam looked at his parents. They were smiling and waving back.

'Bang on time,' said Mr Carnabie. What did he mean, bang on time?

The rider pulled off his leather goggles and helmet, revealing a pink beaming face and a bald domed head, fringed with wiry white hair. As he dismounted, the boy and the girl hinged back the middle section of the sidecar's Perspex canopy and clambered out. The boy, Sam reckoned, was about his own age, the girl maybe a year older. Sam decided that, whoever these people were, he liked them.

'Professor Ampersand!' said Mrs Carnabie, giving the old man a hug.

'It's great to see you!' exclaimed Mr Carnabie, shaking the professor's hand warmly. 'Sam,' he went on, 'this is an old friend, Professor Alexander Ampersand. He attempted to teach applied technology to me and mum when we were at college. He's a remarkable inventor.'

'Delighted to meet you at last, Sam,' said the professor, shaking his hand.

'And this must be your great-niece and great-nephew – Zara and Ben, isn't it?' said Mrs Carnabie.

'That's right,' said Zara.

'Hello,' said Sam, still somewhat perplexed.

'Uncle Alexander built this himself,' said Ben proudly, noticing Sam looking at the motorbike and sidecar.

'Well, I sort of put it together from various bits and

5

pieces,' said the professor, modestly, 'and added one or two wee ideas of my own.'

'Do you want a closer look?' Zara asked Sam.

'Yeah!' Sam walked over to the machine and examined it closely. He could almost feel what it would be like to hurtle along in the sidecar, strapped into one of the seats, which were arranged one behind the other in the long cockpit.

'Professor Ampersand rang us last night, after you'd gone to bed, Sam,' explained Mrs Carnabie.

'We've just been down in London for a couple of days,' said the professor, 'and I thought we'd drop in on our way back home to Edinburgh.'

'When I told the professor that unfortunately we were going away ourselves,' continued Sam's mum, 'and happened to mention that you weren't exactly looking forward to it, he very kindly offered to have you to stay with him and Ben and Zara in Edinburgh for the week.'

'We *were* going to tell you first thing this morning,' said Mr Carnabie. 'But then we thought it'd be fun to save it as a surprise.'

'We'll miss you, of course,' Mrs Carnabie assured Sam. 'But you might have more fun in Edinburgh. It's up to you. What d'you reckon?'

'*I* would,' advised Ben. 'Before they change their mind.'

'We'll have a great time,' promised Zara.

'You really mean it?' Sam asked his parents, a grateful grin breaking across his freckled face.

'You'd better get your bag,' said Mr Carnabie.

Scarcely able to believe his sudden change of fortune, Sam took his rucksack from the Carnabies' hatchback and dropped it into the cockpit of the gleaming yellow sidecar.

Chapter Two

After a quick cup of coffee and a brief exchange of hugs, kisses and phone numbers, they were off. At the main road, the two vehicles parted. Sam gave a last wave to his parents and a last glance at their now vacant back seat as their car disappeared southwards, to pick up the M25 and M4 to Reading. Professor Ampersand opened up the throttle and the motorbike engine gurgled contentedly as they sped northwards to join the M1.

Ben had insisted on giving Sam first turn in the front seat of the sidecar and had made himself a makeshift seat (a toolbox with a folded rug on it) between Sam and Zara.

'The seats swivel round, see?' Ben pointed out. 'So we can talk to each other more easily. You have to lift your knees right up so you've room to turn.'

Sam spun round and faced his new companions.

'Do you live in London?' Sam asked. 'Are you having a holiday with your uncle in Edinburgh?'

'Oh no; we live with Uncle Alexander all the time,' explained Zara. 'He adopted us when our parents were killed in a car crash, when I was two and Ben was one.'

'Oh,' said Sam, wondering if he ought to say he was sorry.

'It's OK,' said Ben. 'It's sad, but we were lucky to have Uncle Alexander. And we don't really remember it happening.'

Sam realized that they'd explained all this to people many times before.

'Uncle Alexander was always Mum's favourite uncle,' said Zara.

'The rest of Mum's family never had much to do with her after she went to work in Tanzania and married Dad,' said Ben, 'even when they came back to Edinburgh and had us.'

'That's sad,' said Sam.

Zara shrugged. 'Their problem. Uncle Alexander's all we need. Anyway,' she continued, breaking the rather serious mood, 'how d'you like travelling by sidecar?'

'It's pretty cool!' answered Sam, enthusiastically. And it was. Sam had never enjoyed a road journey so much before. He enjoyed the scenery rushing past the bubble canopy, making him feel he was flying. He enjoyed the excited looks and waves they got from other drivers and their children. He even enjoyed taking his turn on the toolbox seat, after they'd stopped for lunch and petrol at a motorway service station.

Most of all, though, he enjoyed being with Ben and Zara. They proudly explained the inventions their great-uncle had incorporated into the motorbike and sidecar – the exhaust-heat-recycler which powered the lights, the solar-navigating device which almost worked perfectly as long as you knew what time it was and the sun was out, the gadget on the engine which conserved fuel when the bike was coasting down hills. 'He wants to convert the whole engine to run on hydrogen,' said Zara. 'We were down in London researching it. It's much cleaner than petrol.'

They persuaded Sam to show them his notebook of inventions, they showed him some of their drawings and they chatted away about everything and anything.

Even the weather became more exciting as they got further north – more varied, with a blustery March wind buffeting mountains of cloud across an ever-changing sky; patches of pale sunlight shifting here and there on the hills ahead; occasional showers of rain spitting on their Perspex canopy as they sped on their way. Adventure weather, thought Sam. Just right for an expedition into the unknown.

It was early evening when they finally reached Edinburgh, the city's floodlit domes and spires looking majestic against the darkening sky. They motored west along Princes Street, passing beneath the colossal castle, which seemed to grow out of the rock on which it sat. Sam wondered what kind of house Professor Ampersand and his great-niece and nephew lived in.

Five minutes later, they turned into a short road called Pinkerton Place and slowed down opposite a terrace of ordinary-looking stone-built houses. Professor Ampersand turned the handlebars sharply and, to Sam's alarm, drove directly towards one of the two front windows of the second house from the end, number twelve. Before Sam had time to cry out, the professor pressed a button on the bike's headlamp and instantly the entire window started to slide upwards into the wall above it. At the same time, a metal ramp unfolded itself from the low window sill, clattering across the width of the pavement and onto the road.

As they reached the ramp, a loud explosion interrupted the window's ascent and a shower of blue sparks cascaded from the top of the window frame. With a screech of brakes, the professor brought their vehicle to a violent halt. He leapt from the bike, ran up the ramp, grasped the bottom of the stuck window and shook it vigorously. It shot upwards with the professor still holding on, before reaching its uppermost position with a jolt. Professor Ampersand let go, landed feet first, fell over, performed a rather inelegant backward roll down the ramp and sprang to his feet again in front of the bike.

'That window's always jamming,' he observed, nonchalantly, the last of the blue sparks illuminating his shiny bald head. 'The wood must have swollen up with all the damp weather we've been having. No harm done.'

'NAE HARM DONE! YE CALL IT *NAE HARM* TAE NEARLY ELECTROCUTE THE WHOLE STREET?'

Everyone turned to look at a scrawny, middle-aged man, standing in the doorway of the house next door on the left. He had thinning grey hair, Brylcreemed straight back from his rat-like face.

'Evening, Mr Skinner,' called the Professor, smiling politely. 'Nothing to worry about. Just a wee technical malfunction.'

'THE ONLY TECHNICAL MALFUNCTION IS IN YER *HEID*, YE BARMY AULD BAMPOT!' exploded Mr Skinner, 'YE SHOULD BE LOCKED UP IN ONE O' THEY *MENTAL HAMES*! ENDANGER-ING PUBLIC SAFETY; OBSTRUCTING THE PAVEMENT; LOWERING THE VALUE OF MA PROPERTY WITH YER INFANTILE MACHINES!' He spat contemptuously at the motorbike and sidecar, then stared more closely at the cockpit. At the passengers. At Sam. 'My *god*! Dinnae tell me they've let ye tak on *another* young brat! Ye're no' fit tae look after yersel', never mind yer delinquent weans!'

'Mr Skinner, I think we've heard your offensive views on the children rather too many times before, don't you?' said the professor frostily.

'I'M GOING TAE CALL THE SOCIAL SERVICES AGAIN! I AM!' ranted Mr Skinner. 'IT ISNAE RIGHT, LETTING A WEIRD AULD NUTTER LIKE YOU LOOK AFTER WEANS. IT'S LIKE LIVING NEXT DOOR TAE A *CHILDREN'S HAME!* IT'S –'

'Goodnight, Mr Skinner,' interrupted Professor Ampersand. 'Why don't you go and get yourself some much-needed beauty sleep?' The professor clambered back onto the bike and restarted the engine, drowning out Mr Skinner's reply. They sped up the ramp and in through the now open window of 12 Pinkerton Place.

Chapter Three

It was dark inside the house but, by the light of the head-lamp, Sam could see that the short ramp led them onto a round metal platform standing about half a metre above the floor.

The professor stopped the bike and pressed another button on the headlamp. Almost immediately, the platform spun round so that the bike faced the window through which they had just entered. The ramp outside folded itself back into the windowsill and the window slid shut, this time without getting stuck.

'Don't take any notice of Mr Skinner,' said Zara to Sam. 'He's always like that. His problem.'

Ben hinged back the sidecar's canopy and scrambled out onto the platform. He snapped his fingers twice and the space suddenly became filled with light.

Sam climbed out of the sidecar and looked around. If the outside of the house had looked disappointingly ordinary, the interior more than met his expectations of what an inventor's home ought to look like.

The entire ground floor had been knocked through into one huge room. The space was illuminated by an extraordinary miscellany of lights. Old car lamps and railway lanterns dangled beneath two high metal walk-ways that stretched along the side walls of the room. A chandelier made from old milk bottles gleamed above the far left-hand corner. In the centre of the room, a galaxy of fairy lights spiralled around what appeared to be a bushy green tree, reaching up through a hole in the high ceiling.

'Are the lighting circuits on some sort of sound-activated switch system?' Sam asked Ben. He snapped his fingers twice to test his theory out.

Zara laughed as the room plunged into darkness again. 'Ben was hoping you'd be mystified,' she said, snapping the room back into brightness. 'He tries it on everyone who visits.'

'It's really brilliant, anyway,' Sam said hurriedly.

'You'll not mystify this lad with our wee gimmicks.' Professor Ampersand smiled. 'I can see you're going to be right at home here, Sam.'

Taking their bags from the sidecar, the children followed the professor down from the motorbike platform. To one side of the bike entrance was another front window; to the other side, the front door. Standing beside the door, the professor peeled off his helmet, goggles and gauntlets and removed his coat, revealing a stained, scorched and dilapidated red pullover.

'D'you want to hang your coat up, Sam?' asked the professor. Sam couldn't see any coat hooks until the professor pulled a small lever in the wall. Four brass hooks descended from the ceiling on chains. 'Saves space,' explained the professor, as their four coats sailed upwards and dangled above the front door. 'Come on, let's get some food on.'

Sam could see why space-saving devices were necessary. Down both sides of the room, between the metal pillars supporting the walkways, stood rows of sturdy wooden benches. On one bench, a small rocket appeared to be nearing completion; on another, a machine involving bits of an old grandfather clock and a wind turbine was under construction. Some of the benches were awash with sheets of pencil drawings, diagrams and plans; others supported precarious arrangements of tripods, Bunsen burners and test tubes. Behind the benches, tools of every imaginable and unimaginable variety hung from the walls.

Here and there in the room, a few pieces of everyday furniture made a valiant attempt to re-impose some domestic order on the house: a sofa, armchair and television over by the non-mechanized front window; a dining table and chairs at the back of the room. However, these enclaves of respectable normality were fighting a losing battle with yet more pieces of machinery and incomplete inventions, which spilled out from the workbench areas and sprawled across the wooden floorboards.

The professor was right, Sam decided. He *did* feel at home here. There was something about the sparkle of the fairy lights reflecting magically on glass test tubes; something about the warm glow of the lamps casting mysterious shadows of still more mysterious inventions; something which made Sam's tummy tingle the way it had when he'd first breathed in the smell of the motorbike and sidecar.

In the centre of the back wall, a double French window looked out onto what Sam correctly assumed to be the back garden. Its ornate doors appeared to have been salvaged from two different Victorian greenhouses.

He followed his hosts through an archway to the right of the French windows, into an annexe just about recognizable as a kitchen.

'My oven-boiler heats the house's hot water at the same time as it cooks food,' the professor explained to Sam, pointing to a complex structure that looked like the result of a collision between a historic steam engine and a brass band. The professor slid a switch on the front and, somewhere inside, the gas ignited with a resonant *whoosh*.

'Now, are you partial to the steak-and-kidney pies of Mr Fray and Mr Bentos?' he asked Sam, taking two tins out of a food cupboard.

'Yeah!' said Sam. 'They're my favourite!'

'Mine too,' said the professor, lifting off the lids with a motorized tin opener. 'Now, I think these will cook best in *here* . . .' He deposited one pie into a small door about halfway up the jumble of pipes and compartments . . . 'and *here*.' He opened a second door, slid the other pie in, then frowned. He reached inside and removed the charred remains of what had once been a sausage. 'I was wondering where I'd put that last week,' he said, dropping it into the bin. 'Now, let's have a few tatties.'

He dropped eight muddy potatoes into the top of a cylindrical metal machine which stood on the draining board. The machine whirred noisily for ten seconds, then ejected the cleaned and almost peeled potatoes one at a time. They flew in a graceful arc towards the oven-boiler. Just in time, the professor lifted a round copper lid somewhere in the centre of the structure and six of the potatoes sploshed into a large chamber of steaming water.

'I'll boil some peas in a wee while,' he said, retrieving the two rogue potatoes from the not entirely clean floor and absent-mindedly dropping them into another chamber altogether. 'You three take your bags upstairs. Show Sam where everything is and inflate his dinghy.'

Chapter Four

Ben and Zara led Sam to the fairy-lit column of greenery in the centre of the room, which turned out not to be a tree, but an iron spiral staircase, covered in plant-life. Bushy vines clung around the banisters, baskets of ferns and spider plants hung from the sides and an enormous tropical creeper wound its way up the central pole.

Zara and Ben stopped halfway up the staircase, about two metres from the floor, to show Sam a gate in the banisters.

'See, you can get onto the catwalk,' explained Zara. A thin metal catwalk, with railings on each side, spanned the width of the room, connecting the walkways on each side. Above the walkways, bookshelves filled the wall space up to the ceiling.

'Those are Uncle Alexander's books on that side,' Zara said. 'The ones over there are mine and Ben's.'

They traversed the catwalk across to one library, then to the other, then back to the middle. It was almost like being able to fly and hover over the room, thought Sam. They stood, level with the milk bottle chandelier, looking down over the dining table, along the middle of which the professor had just sent a small clockwork trolley. The trolley was dispensing knives, forks and spoons (more or less in the right order and mostly on the table).

'Come on,' said Zara and they returned to the staircase. They ascended the remaining two metres, through a wide circular stairwell in the high ceiling and crossed a short iron bridge onto the upstairs landing.

'See, the plants grow so well because of all the sunlight they get through the cupola,' said Ben, pointing up to a domed glass skylight which had been built into the roof above them.

They gave Sam a quick tour. Ben's room, with its model aeroplanes hanging from the ceiling, was not unlike Sam's room at home except that every inch of wall space was covered with maps. Antique maps, modern maps, aerial photos and satellite pictures. Maps of Edinburgh, maps of Britain, maps of Europe, Africa, Asia and the Americas. There was even a map of the moon on the ceiling.

'You'll be in here with me, Sam,' said Ben. He dragged a bulky, rolled up bundle of yellow rubber out from beneath his bed and tugged sharply on a red plastic toggle. With a loud PSHHHHHH of compressed air, the bundle rapidly inflated itself into a small life-raft. 'It makes quite a good air-bed,' said Ben, arranging a sleeping bag and pillow into it.

'It's great,' said Sam.

Zara's room was messier than Ben's, mainly because she was halfway through painting a view of the Himalayas on one of her walls. The professor's bedroom was *so* untidy that Sam had to take Ben and Zara's word for it that he actually had a bed somewhere amongst all the piles of books and boxes of papers. The office next to it, by comparison, was surprisingly orderly.

'We have to make him keep it *fairly* tidy,' explained Ben. 'Otherwise he'd never be able to sell any of his ideas or pay any bills or anything.'

'We might as well unpack now,' suggested Zara. 'Oh, the bathroom's there, if you need the loo.'

Sam wasn't surprised to find that the bath was positioned on a raised platform, an arrangement which, as far as he could work out, enabled old bath water to be used to flush the toilet. Nor was he surprised to notice that the shower cubicle had six water-nozzles and three mechanical brushes arranged up and down the inside walls. (He stepped in to have a closer look but stepped out again hurriedly as the brushes began to move automatically.) But he *was* surprised, when he started to wash his hands, to find dozens of tiny green balls cascading out of the hot tap. He yelled and unlocked the door as Ben and Zara came running.

'They're peas!' said Ben. 'Uncle Alexander must have put them into the wrong compartment.' He tasted one. 'Well, at least they're cooked.'

As they finished gathering up the peas into one of Zara's dried-out paint pots, the bathroom window rattled in its frame and a few drops of rain spattered on the pane.

'Come on,' said Zara. 'Let's go down and eat. It's getting late.'

Chapter Five

The pies, the well-travelled peas and the potatoes (mechanically mashed) had all been ravenously devoured, as had the Special Ampersand Exploding Toffee Crumble which the professor had constructed for pudding.

The dishes had been loaded into Professor Ampersand's dishwashing machine and Sam had phoned his parents at Great-Aunt Roberta's to tell them that he'd arrived safely and that everything was brilliant. Now he sat back on the comfortable old sofa, watching TV with Ben and Zara, waiting for a programme about wolves to come on. In the kitchen, the professor could be heard coaxing his labour-saving dishwasher through its task with the odd thump and the occasional 'Och, it shouldn't be doing *that* to the plates.'

A real storm had blown up outside but the sound of the rain lashing down on the skylight only enhanced the feeling of cosiness inside the house.

'It must be really cool living here with Professor Ampersand,' said Sam. 'I mean,' he added quickly, 'it must've been really horrible when your parents were, well, you know, when they died, but, I mean, since then . . .'

'It's all right,' said Zara. 'I know what you mean. We've been really lucky having Uncle Alexander.'

Zara meant what she said. She *was* very happy to have been adopted by her great-uncle. But just occasionally — and she'd never tell this to anyone, not even to Ben and especially not to Uncle Alexander — she did *wonder* what it would be like to have a mother. Someone who'd want to dress her up in really pretty clothes and do her hair and make her feel *glamorous*. Just sometimes.

On the television, the fashion programme preceding their wolf documentary was finishing with an interview with a beautiful blonde woman and her equally attractive husband. They were launching a new range of beauty products.

'We're aiming our Lookin' Good range at the tweenager market,' the woman explained to the presenter, flashing him a perfect white-toothed smile. 'A Lookin' Good Girl will be aged ten to thirteen, a real *peer-group star*, a class-leader personality type – outgoing, popular, the kind of girl who *shines*.'

'Like your own daughter, presumably?' chipped in the presenter.

'Oh, er, absolutely!' said the woman.

'Young people today are so sophisticated,' her husband interjected quickly. 'They're *brand-aware*, *design-conscious* and they want the *best*. The market has to respond to that.'

'Well, I'm sure your new range will be a real success!' gushed the presenter. 'Alicia and Marcus Slick, thanks for coming on the show.'

Zara couldn't help wondering, mostly with curiosity but perhaps with a *tiny* bit of envy, what it would be like to be the daughter of Alicia and Marcus Slick.

As the fashion programme came to an end, Alicia Slick reached out a slim, evenly tanned arm, pointed the brushed-aluminium remote control across her spacious West London living room and switched off the state-of-the-art widescreen television. The interview had been pre-filmed earlier that day and she always liked to monitor her media appearances.

'How did I look?' she asked her husband. 'My chin looked awful, didn't it? I'm going to have to get it *done* again.'

'You looked great, darling,' Marcus assured her.

'I'm getting *neck lines*,' Alicia complained. 'I'm only forty-five and I'm starting to look like an ordinary woman of thirty. It's disgusting.'

'You were *fine*, darling,' said Marcus. '*We* were fine. We look so *good* together. The perfect team.'

Their daughter, Marcia, came into the room.

'Marcia, look at your hair!' exclaimed her mother. 'And what *are* you wearing?'

'Jus' clothes,' said the thirteen-year-old, pushing her tousled brown hair back from her face and looking down at her loose sweatshirt and faded old jeans.

'Where have you been?' asked Alicia.

'Jus' down the park playing football with the gang,' answered Marcia. 'I told you I was getting my tea at Natalie's.'

Alicia winced. 'Not *tea*, darling. *Supper*. And I wish you wouldn't hang around with those people. We don't send you to the most expensive school in Europe so that you can mix with the no-hopers from the local comprehensive.'

'Yeah, well it's the holidays and most of my school friends seem to live in Switzerland, which is a long way to go for a game of football,' retorted Marcia. 'Anyway, I like these friends better.'

'Football was fashionable two years ago,' said Marcus. 'People like us don't have to pretend to like it any more.'

'I'm not pretending to like it,' said Marcia. 'I *do* like it. I'm good at it.'

'You won't make yourself more popular with those urchins by trying to be like them, you know,' insisted Alicia. 'They're bound to be bitching about you behind your back. Making remarks about your nose. Children can be very cruel.'

'*They're* not cruel, they're my friends!' shouted Marcia. 'And there's nothing wrong with my nose!'

'Oh, darling!' laughed Alicia. 'It's terribly sweet of you to pretend not to mind but you know as well as I do that your nose is far too large. And as for your *lips*! . . . I wish you'd have let me book you in with my cosmetic surgeon to get it all fixed two years ago, when I was having my eyelids done.'

'I don't want to look like you!' yelled Marcia. 'I like the way I am!'

'Well, it doesn't matter now, anyway,' Marcus interrupted, giving his wife a warning glance. 'Everything will be sorted out soon.'

'Oh yes, that's right,' said Alicia.

'What do you mean, "everything will be sorted out soon"?' demanded Marcia, suspiciously.

'Oh, nothing, darling,' cooed her mother. 'Nothing you need to worry about. Your father and I have got everything in hand and soon we'll be the perfect happy family we've always wanted to be.'

Chapter Six

'Time you three were getting ready for bed,' observed Professor Ampersand, as the wolf programme came to an end. He was sitting in the armchair next to the children now, attempting to glue pieces of dinner plate back together with his experimental porcelain adhesive.

'All right,' yawned Zara, 'I'll just . . .'

BRRRRRING! The doorbell rang loudly, followed immediately by a frantic thumping on the front door.

'Whoever's that at this time of night?' wondered the professor as he walked to the door (with several pieces of plate glued firmly to the bottom of his jacket). The children followed him.

BRRRRRRRRRRING!! The bell's harsh ringing continued, as did the increasingly desperate hammering, until the professor opened the door.

A tall, bedraggled figure blew into the room on a gust of wind and rain and staggered over to the nearest work bench. He leant against it, clearly exhausted and soaked to the skin, desperately trying to remain standing.

'Eric!' exclaimed Professor Ampersand, hurrying to support him.

From beneath the wide brim of his sodden leather hat, the stranger's bony, age-creviced face wore a haunted expression. From their deep, dark sockets, his pale grey eyes stared at the open front door.

'Am I being followed, Alexander?' he rasped, weakly. 'Look outside, quickly!'

Professor Ampersand peered this way and that through the sheets of rain before closing the door, with some difficulty, against the storm. 'No one, as far as I can see,' he reported. 'But, Eric, let me help you off with these wet clothes and . . .'

'Listen!' croaked the man. 'Can't . . stay . . awake . . much . . longer . . . Summon the others, Alexander . . . *Professor Murdo has returned to Nordbergen.*'

For a few seconds neither man spoke. The children stared at the stranger. He was hardly able to stand now. Water dripped from his long coat to form a puddle around his battered walking boots.

'Good lord,' said Professor Ampersand, quietly.

'I know what he's doing,' breathed the man, weakly. 'Know what he's trying to do . . . *And he's close, Alexander . . . Too close . . .*' He began to fall forward as his legs gave way beneath him.

'Eric, are you injured? Or sick?' cried Professor Ampersand, catching him.

'No . . . exhausted . . . No sleep . . . many days . . . many, many days,' the stranger rambled.

'Do you need food?' asked the professor, clearly much concerned. 'Ben, Zara, get a hot bath running and –'

'No. Sleep first . . . Wake me . . . when . . . others . . . arrive . . . *Summon the others . . . Summon the others . . .*'

Together, Professor Ampersand and Ben somehow managed to manhandle the semiconscious man up the spiral staircase and into the professor's office. Zara and Sam hastily assembled a spare camp bed on which their mysterious visitor was at last able to surrender himself to sleep.

'I'd have put him on the sofa downstairs but he's going to need to sleep on undisturbed tomorrow,' said the professor. 'I'll take his wet clothes off in a minute and put a couple of quilts over him. But first I must e-mail the others.'

Bursting with questions, the three children stood around the computer whilst Professor Ampersand sent the same message to four different addresses:

Eric is here. News of Murdo. Come at once. Urgent.
Alexander. x

'There!' said Professor Ampersand. 'Now it really is time you three were getting ready for b–'

'You can't send us to bed now!' protested Zara. 'Not without telling us what's going on! Who is this man?'

'And who's Professor Murdo?' asked Ben, 'And who are *the others*?'

The professor thought for a moment. 'All right,' he said. 'Get into your pyjamas and brush your teeth whilst I sort out Eric here with some bedding. Then I'll tell you the whole story before you go to sleep.'

Chapter Seven

'There were seven of us,'
began Professor Ampersand,

'Myself,
Professor Eric Gauntraker, whom you've just met,
Professor Roderick Murdo, of whom you heard Eric
 speak,
and the four people I've just e-mailed:
Professor Ivy Sharpe,
Professor Garrulous Gadling,
Professor Petunia Hartleigh-Broadbeam and
Professor Bob Pottle.'

Professor Ampersand looked surprisingly comfortable, his long body somehow folded into (or mostly out of) the child's armchair in the corner of Ben's bedroom, his lined face bathed in the warm glow of the illuminated globe which served as a bedside lamp. Sam and Ben sat up in their beds and Zara sat on the end of Ben's bed in her dressing gown.

'Thirty-five years ago, we were all members of the Edinburgh Scientists, Inventors and Explorers Society, an organization of about sixty people who met once a month to have dinner and discuss new ideas, inventions, expeditions etc. At one such club dinner, our chairwoman read out a rather unusual open invitation that our society had received from the people of Nordbergen. Nordbergen is a small island, about the size of the Isle of Wight, situated well inside the Arctic Circle, in the Barents Sea, round about . . . *here.*' The professor indicated a position on Ben's globe.

'The other islands in the region,' he continued, 'are owned by Norway and Russia but, perhaps because of Nordbergen's smallness, neither country had ever bothered to claim it and the Nordbergers had enjoyed a relatively independent existence for centuries. The Nordbergers were descended from a rich mix of Sami, Scandinavians, Samoyeds, Slavs, Inuits and a good many others, a mixture reflected in their remarkable language.

'At this point in their history, the Nordbergers were finding it hard to make a living from fishing and hunting. The island's young people had to leave Nordbergen to complete their education and find work. It's a beautiful part of the world to live in, but a hard one too. Although the sun doesn't set for months on end in summer, the winter brings permanent darkness and the sea freezes into a vast plain of ice.

'However, under the leadership of their young leader, Thor Pietronaq, the Nordbergers hit upon a scheme which they hoped would reverse their island's fortunes. They decided to create the best university in the world. It wasn't as far-fetched an idea as it might sound. Nordbergen's location offered endless new research opportunities for ecologists, biologists, astronomers, oceanographers, scientists of every field, as well as inspiration for composers, artists and writers. They planned to invite people from all over the world to participate in this venture. The university would revitalize the island's economy and provide education and employment for their young people.

'Due to an old friendship between our society's chair-woman and a Nordbergen elder, our organization was the first to be approached. As I said, there were seven of us to

27

whom this seemed like a great opportunity. To Eric Gauntraker, Nordbergen would be the ideal base for Arctic exploration. Ivy Sharpe, an environmental biologist, planned to research the ecology of the Arctic seas. Garrulous Gadling, a naturalist and explorer, was determined to discover new species up there in the frozen wastes. Petunia Hartleigh-Broadbeam, Bob Pottle and myself, all inventors, planned to research wind and wave energy sources – that was, once we persuaded Bob to drop his original idea of researching walrus dung as a viable fuel for motor cars.

'Roderick Murdo was rather secretive about the work he planned to do, saying only that it was of immense benefit to the future of mankind. He was a brilliant scientist in many disciplines, always striving to be the best in any field he entered, but not an easy man to get to know well.

'So, we were to become the founding professors of the new University of Nordbergen. The other members of the Society nicknamed us the Seven Professors of the Far North.

'Among Professor Murdo's many qualifications, he held a pilot's licence. He owned an old DC-3 – a twin-engined passenger and cargo plane – and he offered to fly us and our equipment up to Nordbergen. He'd restored the plane beautifully, polishing its silvery surface and even painting his family emblem of a raven's head on each side of the tail fin. On a more practical level, Petunia and I adapted the under-carriage so it could switch from wheels to skis, for landing on ice. We assembled our supplies and, one bright morning in early spring, the heavily laden plane lifted into the sky. It was a beautiful flight, first over the cold blue water of the North Sea, then up the long, craggy coastline of Norway and finally over the endless tracts of ice to the small island at the top of the world that was to be our new home.

'At first everything went well. We planned our research programmes, timetabled our teaching schedules for the first students (who were due to arrive in September) and worked enthusiastically on the construction of the new buildings, near the island's main town, Oskvik. Our University campus was little more than a cluster of Portakabins surrounding a semi-ruined castle, but to our eyes it was grander than the grandest spires of Oxford or Cambridge. The hospitality of the Nordbergers was as warm as the place was cold and we worked day and night with them in a great spirit of hope and camaraderie.

'But then Professor Murdo began to cause problems. He demanded that the most substantial of the buildings – the keep of the old castle – should be given to him for his exclusive use as a laboratory. He still refused to disclose the nature of his planned work but he claimed that his project was far more important than our silly little experiments. Then he insisted that our planned expansion of the University, to bring in many more scientists, as well as artists and so on, was pointless. Effectively, he wanted to turn the entire University into his own private research centre.'

'So what did you do?' asked Zara. 'Did you kick him out?'

'We didn't want to antagonize him if we could avoid it,'

answered Professor Ampersand. 'His academic reputation was a tremendous asset to our fledgling university, not to mention his aeroplane. We decided to allow him to work undisturbed in the old keep for the time being and simply ignore everything else he said, hoping his sullen mood would blow over.

'However, before long, matters were brought to a head. One night, a month or so after we'd first arrived, a group of twenty fur-clad islanders burst into our Portakabin staff room, in a state of extreme anger and agitation. One young woman in particular seemed absolutely hysterical. These weren't islanders directly connected to the University project but people from one of Nordbergen's few remaining fishing villages, on the remote eastern peninsula. They were all speaking so fast that not even Eric, who had begun to master the Nordbergers' complex language, could understand them properly. But two words they kept repeating were clear enough: *Professor Murdo*.

'As usual, Professor Murdo was working late, alone in his laboratory. We flung on our outdoor clothing and began to take the villagers across to the keep, though by the time we reached it they had overtaken us and were hammering on the locked wooden door, the young woman screaming angrily the whole time. Failing to gain entry with their fists or shoulders, the villagers found a huge wooden rafter from the ruined part of the castle and rammed the door down. We burst into the large room. Professor Murdo was there all right, standing defiantly behind a stainless steel table, in the far corner. And there, on the table we could all see what it was that Professor Murdo had that was so distressing the young woman.'

'*What was it?*' asked Ben. 'What did he have?

'Her baby,' said Professor Ampersand, quietly. 'He had her baby.'

Chapter Eight

'Her *baby!*' exclaimed Ben. 'How had he got her baby?'

'We discovered later that he'd driven out to the fishing village in the University snowmobile and simply snatched the ten-month-old boy from his mother by force,' said Professor Ampersand. 'As it turned out, the baby was unharmed, though heavily sedated. But the sinister array of syringes and scalpels laid out on the steel table suggested that we'd interrupted him not a moment too soon.'

'But what was he going to do to the baby?' asked Sam.

'We never found out,' Professor Ampersand replied. 'As we burst in, Professor Murdo looked past the mother and the crowd of villagers as if they didn't exist and fixed us, his six colleagues, with a terrible stare of anger, contempt and disbelief. "*Betrayed!*" he cried. "*You've betrayed me to this rabble of primitive savages!*" Then, as we surged forward across the room, he seized a large chemical-filled bottle from the shelves behind him, stuffed a handkerchief from his pocket into the top, set light to it and flung his makeshift incendiary onto a cluttered wooden desk. With a crash of exploding glass, Professor Murdo's papers, chemicals and equipment were engulfed in a huge ball of fire. The young woman reached her baby just in time and fled with him back to the door we'd come through. Those of us who had almost reached Professor Murdo were driven back as more chemical jars exploded in the heat. Through the flames we saw him disappear through a small doorway at the back of the room.

'But there was no time to chase Murdo now. We had to evacuate the keep, and fast. Outside, dozens of Nordbergers, led by Thor Pietronaq, were rushing to the burning castle with fire-fighting equipment. But it was no good. In the brisk Arctic wind, the fire spread with merciless speed. Burning debris from the old castle fell and blew onto the Portakabins. Before long, it was clear that all we could do was retreat to a safe distance across the snow-covered ground and watch our beloved University go up in flames. You can imagine how we felt.

'Then some more men came running up from the town with news of another blow which had befallen Nordbergen. Whilst most of the population had been out fighting the fire, someone had broken into the Government Treasury Office, knocked two guards unconscious, blown open the safe and stolen most of the Nordbergers' reserves of money and gold. It wasn't difficult to guess who the culprit might be but, before we had time to go and investigate, a sound cut through the air; a sound we should have been expecting – the harsh clatter of the DC-3's twin engines bursting into life.

'"To the airstrip!" roared Eric, leaping onto Thor's two-man skidoo. My other four colleagues and I clung on as best we could and we sped recklessly to the flat piece of ground a quarter of a mile uphill from the University. There, parked badly in front of the aircraft hangar was the University snowmobile. The hangar doors were open and the large, silver aeroplane stood gleaming in the floodlights, its powerful engines blasting clouds of snow back across the ice-covered runway. It seemed poised to take off. Yet it wasn't moving. And the cargo door, in the rear of one side of the fuselage, was still open. Maybe Professor Murdo was still loading up. Maybe we were still in time to stop him! We hurtled up to the plane . . .

'Crack! Something hit hard into the front of our skidoo, cutting our engine dead. Professor Murdo sprang down from the passenger door of the DC-3, pointing a modern, military-looking rifle straight at us. "Get in the cargo hold!" he shouted above the engines' deafening noise. "No one will listen to the ignorant inhabitants of this godforsaken island but I'm not leaving you six to blab about my work!" Briskly, he shepherded us at gunpoint in through the cargo door, which he locked behind us. Through the strong metal grille that separated our windowless section of the plane from the main passenger cabin we could see the Nordbergers' stolen strongbox, lying on the floor between the passenger seats. Professor Murdo climbed swiftly back into the cockpit and, in less than a minute, the DC-3 was roaring up into the night sky, leaving Nordbergen far behind.

'We tried everything to break through the metal grille but our efforts were in vain. Two and a half hours later, as the plane began to descend, we were still prisoners. We felt the bump of skis on ice as we landed and slid to a halt. Leaving the engines running, Professor Murdo stood in the cockpit doorway, aiming his rifle at us. "Thanks to you traitors, Nordbergen is finished," he growled, "but my work will continue. I am the future! You puny fools are history. For you, this journey is over." Without taking his gun or his eyes off us, he reached into the cockpit behind him and pulled a lever. With a clunk, the cargo door slid open and a blast of icy air rushed into the already chilly hold. We looked out into the dark. Not a light shone anywhere. Not a single sign of life, human or otherwise. Just mile after mile of endless ice. "Get out," ordered Professor Murdo. "One by one. Each person is to walk five hundred paces from the plane before the next person goes. No funny business outside the plane or I'll shoot whoever's left. You first, Eric. Move! Or I'll shoot all of you."

'We obeyed him. What else could we do? Obviously, that far from anywhere, in those conditions, without food, equipment or proper expedition clothing, our chances of survival were almost zero, but it was that or be shot. He kept his gun trained on us until all six of us were standing five hundred yards from the plane, huddled together for warmth. Then he returned to his seat, opened up the engines to full power and took off. We watched in silence as the lights of the DC-3 disappeared into the starry sky.'

'But if he was leaving you to die on the ice anyway,' asked Zara, 'why didn't he just shoot you?'

''Cos shooting would leave evidence,' suggested Sam.

'I think that's right,' agreed Professor Ampersand. 'There was always a remote chance that our bodies would be discovered and I suppose he realized that any bullets could link our deaths to him.'

'Whereas if you'd frozen to death, there'd be no evidence of anything,' said Ben.

'But how *did* you survive?' asked Zara. 'How come you *didn't* all freeze to death or starve?'

For a moment, Professor Ampersand sat in silence, the tips of his long fingers pressed together in front of his chin. 'Zara,' he said at last, 'you know I never keep secrets from you and Ben. If I could, I'd tell you both the whole story, and Sam too, of course. But the explanation of how we returned home safely involves a secret that is not my secret to tell. It was Professor Gauntraker who knew of it. A secret that had been passed on to him by his grand-mother, also a remarkable explorer in her time. *One of the most extraordinary secrets in the world.* And even in our perilous situation in the icy wilderness, Eric only agreed to use this knowledge to save us if we first all promised never to tell another living soul or use the secret ourselves, without his permission.'

'But, Uncle . . .' persisted Zara.

Professor Ampersand held up a hand. 'I'm sorry,' he said, gently, 'but a promise is a promise. And you'd better not go pestering Eric about this either. Maybe I've already said too much. Anyway,' he continued, breaking the frustrated silence, 'suffice it to say that we returned safely to Edinburgh. We immediately contacted the Nordbergers, who were relieved to hear that we were alive but had little else to be cheerful about. With their funds stolen, the buildings burnt to the ground and growing local hostility towards the whole idea of the University, the Nordberger government had to abandon its plans altogether. Over the next five years, the population continued to dwindle until eventually the few remaining Nordbergers were left with no choice but to evacuate their homeland and resettle in various parts of Northern Europe.

'To this day Nordbergen has remained uninhabited, or so I'd believed. The six of us have kept in touch over the

Chapter Nine

Sam lay awake in the comfortable dinghy bed, just able to make out the shadowy form of the model biplane above him.

'A concealed mobile phone, to call for help?' suggested Ben's voice through the darkness.

'They didn't have mobile phones then,' pointed out Zara's voice, sounding tinny through the homemade intercom link from her bedroom. 'Or satellites to relay the signal. And even if it *was* that, why would it still be a secret?'

'What about a secret air base, near to where they were left stranded?' tried Sam. 'Known only to polar explorers.'

'Better,' conceded Ben. 'But even that wouldn't still be *such* a big secret. Not one of the most extraordinary secrets in the world.'

The mystery raised by Professor Ampersand's story might have kept Sam, Ben and Zara awake for hours. But it had been a long day and in the silence, as each child racked their brains for another solution worth suggesting to the others, they somehow fell asleep.

It was just as well they slept while they could, for at six o'clock the following morning, they were woken by the ringing of the front doorbell. This wasn't the frantic, melodramatic ringing and hammering of the night before but a single, controlled ring, sustained for five seconds precisely. It was the sort of ring that knows it will have to wake the household but believes it to be the household's fault for not being up yet.

The children came halfway down the stairs in their pyjamas and watched from the catwalk as Professor Ampersand, wearing a long velvet dressing gown, opened the front door. 'Good morning, Ivy!' he said as a petite woman in her early sixties stepped into the house. She wore a simple, high-necked fawn jacket and matching trousers, tucked into white leather ankle boots. Her grey hair was cut in a neat, almost geometric bob which framed a slim, rather angular face. On her back she carried a small silvery-grey haversack.

'It's good to see you,' exclaimed Professor Ampersand, giving Professor Sharpe a hug and a kiss on the cheek, 'You got here very quickly. You must only have got my e-mail a few hours ago.'

'It was extremely inconvenient,' said Professor Sharpe. 'I was in the middle of organizing a United Nations bio-diversity conference in Geneva when I got your e-mail on my micro-laptop. But your message said to come at once so I came at once. I arranged for a colleague to cover for me and took a flight to Amsterdam in time to catch the 04.15 flight to Edinburgh, obviously prearranging for a taxi to meet me. I take it then that I'm the first to arrive? Where's Eric?'

'Fast asleep,' Professor Ampersand told her. 'It'd take more than the doorbell to wake him just now. We'll leave him sleeping till the others arrive. But I see that Zara, Ben and Sam are awake,' he added, looking up at the catwalk, 'so I'll get some breakfast on.'

After breakfast (bacon, eggs and an accidentally machine-fried banana for Professor Ampersand and the children; a handful of bran-flakes and an apple for Professor Sharpe), Professor Ampersand decided to have another go at making his dishwasher work properly, while Professor Sharpe caught up with some work on her laptop. Zara and Ben took Sam out into the back garden to show him the micro-scooter roller-coaster they were building. The storm had blown itself out during the night and the rain had subsided to a fine drizzle.

Just before lunchtime the doorbell rang again (this time with a cheerful *brri-brrring!*) and the children ran into the house to see Professor Ampersand warmly greeting two more visitors, a man and a woman, both in their late sixties.

The man's pear-shaped figure, large beaky nose and double chin gave him a curiously pelican-like appearance. He wore a crumpled cream suit, a polka-dotted red bow tie and a panama hat. He put down his battered brown holdall and shook the children's hands in turn. 'Garrulous Gadling!' he boomed. 'And you must be Zara, Ben and . . . um . . .'

'This is Sam,' said Professor Ampersand. 'Sam Carnabie.' He turned to the woman. 'And this is Professor Petunia Hartleigh-Broadbeam.'

Professor Hartleigh-Broadbeam was a large, striking woman. Her attire was a unique combination of the glamorous (a pink flowery jacket), the practical (an oil-stained grey boiler suit) and the distinctive (a tweed deer-stalker hat, worn with the earflaps down over her wispy blonde hair). 'Simply *delicious* to meet you, m'dears,' she declared, smiling at the children. 'And how well *you're* looking, Alexander. Garrulous and I bumped into one another on the train and took a taxi here together. We'd have been here sooner but the wretched train was delayed. Of course if the authorities would listen to *me* and adopt my solar-powered monorail solution . . . but there we go. They think all us inventors are mad scientists! Eccentric crackpots! It makes me so angry. I blame the media, as I was saying to Sherlock as I put him on this morning. Ah, Ivy, so you're here already . . .'

'Who's Sherlock?' whispered Zara to Professor Ampersand.

'Her deerstalker hat,' he whispered back. 'She gives all her hats names. You should see Davy. Real racoon skin. Stripy tail, glass eyes and everything.'

'Lucky I was in the country when your e-mail came through, Alexander,' said Professor Gadling, tucking into the pizza Professor Ampersand had made for lunch. 'I'm off to Brazil next week to photograph the Parrot-Eating Octopus of Amazonia.'

'Oh, don't be ridiculous!' snapped Professor Sharpe. 'There's no such species!'

'Of course there is!' declared Professor Gadling. 'But it's very rare.'

'How does it catch parrots?' asked Sam, not sure who to believe.

'It leaves its muddy river home and climbs right to the top of the trees,' explained Professor Gadling. 'Then it finds a gap in the forest canopy and grips its two front tentacles on to some high branches. With its remaining six tentacles it pulls its body back down to the forest floor, stretching the front tentacles to a simply enormous length.'

'Not as far as you're stretching our credulity,' sniped Professor Sharpe.

'A Parrot-Eating Octopus might wait for hours or even days, staring up at the space through the treetops,' Professor Gadling went on, ignoring the heckle, 'until, eventually, a flock of parrots flies high overhead. Then it releases the grip of its rear tentacles and *boing!* it catapults itself straight up into the sky, bang into the centre of the flock, taking the parrots completely by surprise. It lashes out its tentacles with deadly accuracy, sometimes catching as many as eight parrots in a single raid. It catches them by the feet of course, so that the parrots' flapping wings brake the octopus's descent. Then it drowns them in the river and eats them.'

'Total nonsense!' snorted Professor Sharpe.

'Total scientific fact!' insisted Professor Gadling. 'You believe me, don't you?' he appealed to the children. The three of them looked at each other, all wanting Professor Gadling to be right, yet none of them wanting Professor Sharpe to think them foolish.

'Well, what happens if the octopus misses and doesn't catch any parrots?' asked Ben. 'Wouldn't he come down too fast?'

'Absolutely!' agreed Professor Gadling. 'He comes down so fast, the fall kills him. Splat! But of course those octopuses with poor aim don't survive to pass on their genes so, over the millennia, the species has evolved a pretty high success rate. A perfect example of the Survival Of The Fittest principle.'

'A perfect example of *absolute rubbish*!' cried Professor Sharpe.

'Well, isn't this lovely? All of us together again,' observed Professor Hartleigh-Broadbeam. 'All except Bob Pottle. Didn't you say he was on his way?'

'Bob e-mailed me this morning,' said Professor Ampersand, 'to say he'd be here before lunch. He's only coming from Middlesborough so I'm surprised he's not here yet.'

'He's probably travelling in a urine-powered car which he's built himself and has broken down,' said Professor Sharpe.

'That's a *bit* unkind,' said Professor Ampersand. 'Bob's inventions aren't *that* bad.'

Sam, Ben and Zara spent a pleasant afternoon working on the roller-coaster with Professor Ampersand and Professor Hartleigh-Broadbeam (ignoring the scowls from Mr Skinner's kitchen window), while Professor Gadling regaled them with tales of the African Hunting Bat, the Madagascan Frisbee Moth and the Killer Pygmy Panda of Sarawak.

Darkness fell and the drizzling rain gave way to a thick fog, a real east-coast haar, Professor Gadling said. As they came inside, the doorbell rang (just once and briefly).

'Bob! At last!' said Professor Ampersand to the small, pale-skinned man who stood on the doorstep. 'Come in, come in.'

Professor Bob Pottle shuffled into the room. He wore a badly-fitting raincoat over brown corduroy trousers. He peered at the assembled company through his round spectacles and rubbed his rather unsuccessful beard nervously. 'Sorry I'm – erm – a bit behind my estimated time of arrival,' he said. 'Had a bit of trouble with my new urine-powered car. Can't understand it. Perfectly sound in principle. Had to leave it on the A184 and get a bus into Newcastle. Caught a train from there but it – erm – turned out to be coming *from* Edinburgh, instead of going *to* it. Didn't stop until Darlington and then I missed the 13:27 back because they hadn't numbered the platforms clearly. Had to wait for the 16:06. I walked here from Waverley Station but your street isn't where my compass said it should be at all. Most odd. Can I use your loo?'

'I'll take you up,' offered Professor Ampersand, 'and I'll wake Eric. He can tell us why he's summoned you all here whilst we eat. It's time to find out what he's discovered.'

Chapter Ten

In the gleaming light of the milk-bottle chandelier, they sat around the long dining table, as Professor Ampersand served up nine steaming platefuls of goulash and rice. He sat with the three children down one side of the table. Professor Sharpe, Professor Pottle and Professor Gadling sat down the other side and Professor Hartleigh-Broadbeam sat at the far end, near the French windows. All eyes were on the spiral staircase as Professor Gauntraker finally descended into the room. After twenty hours' sleep, a shower and a shave, he looked considerably less haggard than the night before, though his face still carried a haunted expression. 'Good evening,' he said, taking his place at the head of the table. Wasting no further words on greetings, he gave his full attention to the plate of food in front of him, shovelling a dozen large forkfuls into his mouth without a pause. 'My apologies,' he growled in a gravelly voice, 'but I have eaten very little for many days, since I escaped from Nordbergen.'

'You've come from Nordbergen?' asked Professor Pottle. 'Did you use the – erm – *secret method*?'

'No! I was being pursued by Murdo's security forces on long-range snowmobiles and I couldn't risk leading them straight to it.' Professor Gauntraker stopped, noticing Sam, Ben and Zara's attentive expressions. 'And I might remind you all,' he continued sternly, 'that we must not discuss the Great Secret in the presence of anyone else.'

'Oh – erm – quite,' said Professor Pottle.

'Absolutely!' agreed Professor Ampersand, giving the children a sidelong glance.

'However, before we close the subject,' continued Professor Gauntraker, 'I *will* tell you that I have prepared instructions for using the secret to return to the Far North; instructions which I keep concealed about my person. I *may* decide later to pass these on to one of you, just in case anything happens to me.'

'What do you mean, Eric, in case anything happens to you?' asked Professor Hartleigh-Broadbeam, anxiously. 'Are you still being followed?'

'One can never be totally sure,' stated Professor Gauntraker. 'However, I'm reasonably certain that I gave my pursuers the slip in the icy inlets of the White Sea. But I took no chances. I dumped my stolen snowmobile and hid out with a group of Sami reindeer herdsmen for a few days. I managed to slip into Finland and travelled by dog sled across Lapland to Northern Sweden, living off the land and passing myself off as a Norwegian trapper. (As you know, I speak twenty-three languages fluently.) I finally reached Norway, where I made my way down the coast, avoiding large towns. Murdo's men were bound to be watching the ferry ports so I traded my dog sled for an unobtrusive sailing dinghy and set out across the North Sea.

'Halfway across, disaster struck. A gale blew up and my mainsail was badly torn. Then a freak wave swept the last of my food supplies overboard. Luckily, a flock of herring gulls flew close to the dinghy, swooping onto my lost food. Using a technique I once learned when living among the Cree of Ontario, I managed to snare the largest gull in a loop of fishing twine.'

'Wow!' said Zara, impressed. 'And did you catch the whole flock and get them to pull you across the sea?'

'Don't be ridiculous,' said Professor Gauntraker. 'I wrung the gull's neck and plucked its carcass. By careful rationing, the meat just kept me alive until my damaged dinghy finally reached the Scottish coast, near Fraserburgh.'

'Urgh!' exclaimed Ben. 'You *ate* raw seagull?'

'Believe me, lad,' uttered Professor Gauntraker, 'when you're 150 miles from land, facing starvation in an open boat in a force nine gale, raw seagull flesh tastes like the finest banquet you've ever eaten. No disrespect to your excellent cooking, Alexander,' he added, shovelling in another mouthful of goulash. 'Anyway,' he continued. 'I managed to hitchhike most of the way south to Edinburgh, travelling incognito, of course, as an itinerant farm labourer. But I had to complete the last twelve miles on foot.'

'These traveller's tales are all very impressive, Eric,' said Professor Sharpe, sipping her wine, 'but you haven't told your story from the beginning. *How* did you find Professor Murdo on Nordbergen and what is he *doing* there?'

'To the crux of the matter as always, Ivy,' acknowledged Professor Gauntraker. 'I went to Nordbergen to investigate a rumour I'd heard from an old Arctic trapper that aircraft had been seen landing on the island. Strange, almost silent aircraft which carried no registration numbers or national markings, but only the emblem of a raven's head.'

'Professor Murdo's family emblem!' remembered Sam.

'Precisely. To cut a long story short, I discovered that a ring of security now surrounds Nordbergen: an entire garrison of heavily armed mercenaries equipped with aircraft, snow-mobiles, radar, surveillance cameras – you name it. However, I eventually made it onto the island and infiltrated Murdo's headquarters and, before I was discovered and pursued, I found out *exactly* what Professor Murdo has been working on for the past thirty-five years or more. *If he succeeds, it will be the end of human life as we know it.* And he's close to succeeding. Very close. Too close.'

The other professors and the three children leant forward in rapt attention as Professor Gauntraker finished his last forkful. 'What Professor Murdo is attempting to do,' he continued, 'is to . . . *My God!*'

He stopped suddenly, staring past them all at the French windows, his eyes wide with alarm. Eight heads spun round to follow his gaze. Almost silently, the shadowy, geometric form of a strange aircraft was dropping vertically through the fog, into the back garden.

'*My God!*' repeated Professor Gauntraker breathlessly. '*They've found me!*'

A sudden flash of white flame erupted from the front of the aircraft and the French windows blasted inwards, shattered glass flying everywhere. Instantly, amid the cries of alarm, Professor Ampersand raised a hand and snapped the room into blackness. 'Zara, Ben, Sam!' he hissed. '*Hide!*'

Sam slipped from his chair feeling Ben pulling his arm, whispering frantically: '*This way!*' Then Zara's voice: '*No, over here!*' Ouch! Someone's chair. Where was Ben now? A sudden white light. Quick, under the table! No – too exposed. The spiral staircase.

'*FREEZE!*'

PKKKKKZZZZSSTT! Harsh, flickering light behind him. What was that? Don't look back – under the plants – up the steps – keep low – stop here. Keep still.

Gasping for breath, heart thumping, Sam peered carefully through the foliage-covered banisters. Had he been seen? Where were Ben and Zara? From the centre of the aircraft, a powerful searchlight penetrated the fog, capturing the room in its icy glare. Three black-clad figures, balaclavas masking all but their eyes, stood inside the doorway, brandishing large black guns. Professor Hartleigh-Broadbeam was covered in shards of glass, blood trickling from one side of her face. 'I SAID *FREEZE!*' roared the tallest intruder. He was pointing his gun not at Sam, but at Professor Sharpe, who was clutching her right hand. The charred remains of a mobile phone lay smouldering at her feet. '*Hands on heads! All of you! NOW!*' The six professors obeyed.

Suddenly, Sam heard a splintering crack behind him, from the front of the house. Someone was breaking in through the front door. The newcomer strode across the room to the others, passing within a metre of Sam's hiding place. He too wore a tight black combat suit but no balaclava. The right shoulder of his black jacket, Sam noticed, bore a small emblem: the silhouette of a raven's head within a silver circle. His piggy face, topped by a bristly crew-cut and adorned with a thin blond moustache, smirked with satisfaction. 'Good work, sergeant,' he said to the tall gunman. 'Looks like we bagged ourselves the full set.'

'No one else?' checked the sergeant. 'No kids or nuffing upstairs?'

Sam's heart leapt into his throat. Should he attempt to move?

'No. Ampersand's not married,' said the blond man. 'We checked. Right, let's get 'em into the plane. One at a time.'

'This is outrageous!' protested Professor Hartleigh-Broadbeam as one of the men fastened her wrists together behind her back and marched her at gunpoint towards the shattered French windows. 'Who are you?'

'Your pal Gauntraker here should've introduced me, darling,' smirked the blond man. 'Major Nigel Smedling, head of security at Nordbergen Research Enterprises.'

'I could have sworn you hadn't succeeded in following me here,' growled Professor Gauntraker, as Professor Gadling was also led away.

'Didn't need to, granddad,' said Major Smedling. 'We fired a Micro-Tracking Device onto your hat as you left Nordbergen. Been following your progress by satellite ever since. Gave us a good laugh, watching you play cowboys and Indians across Scandinavia for no purpose at all. Soon as you arrived here, we checked this address and it all fell into place. The boss gave me the complete list and we simply waited for you all to turn up. I've been watching the house from the bottom of the road all day.'

'Where are you taking us?' demanded Professor Pottle as his wrists were fastened behind him.

'Nordbergen, of course,' replied the Major. 'The boss is just dying to meet you all again after all these years, though you'll have to wait until Wednesday, when he returns from a business trip. After you've had your reunion, we've got a nice little diving expedition organized for you. Through a hole in the ice. Bit cold, of course, but you'll be wearing leaded boots to keep your feet warm.'

'You'll never get away with this!' snapped Professor Sharpe as she was led out. 'Your aircraft will be spotted by the whole neighbourhood! And by air traffic control!'

'This plane, darling,' boasted Major Smedling, 'is the last word in low-audibility, vertical-take-off, radar-invisible stealth technology. And if any of the neighbours *do* spot us through this fog, I don't think the police are going to waste too much time on reports of a UFO landing in an Edinburgh back garden, do you?'

'No,' said Professor Gauntraker, slowly. 'There'd be no point in anyone going to the police.' Professor Gauntraker was standing with his back to Sam's hiding place on the staircase. As he spoke, Sam saw him grip the cuff button on the left sleeve of his old brown jacket. He gripped it between the index and middle fingers of his right hand, all

48

the time keeping both hands on the back of his head. He gave a sharp tug and the button broke loose and bounced from his shoulders down to the floor.

'Right, we'll take these last two together,' ordered Major Smedling and without any further talking, Professor Gauntraker and Professor Ampersand were manacled and led out. Professor Ampersand's eyes were filled with anxiety but he did nothing that might have given the children away.

His head burning with fear and helplessness, Sam watched the men disappear through the mist, until they were swallowed up into the mysterious silhouette of the aircraft. He heard the soft thud of a door closing in the side of the plane. The floodlight went out and the sombre shape rose into the murky night sky, its soft, menacing roar fading to nothing. The cold fog drifted into the dark room and there was silence.

Chapter Eleven

Zara was the first to speak. 'Have all the men gone?' her voice hissed from the shadows behind one of the work-benches.

'I think so,' croaked Sam. His throat was dry and his heart was still pounding. Gingerly, he made his way down the staircase. Through the darkness, he could just see Zara moving quickly to a shelf beside the kitchen doorway. He heard the rattle of the telephone receiver being lifted.

'The phone's dead!' said Zara. 'They must have cut the line somehow, before they attacked. Come on! The phone box by the shop up the road . . . we must phone the police.' In spite of her decisive manner, her voice trembled.

As Zara crossed the room towards the front door, Ben emerged from behind another bench. He reached up his right hand but before he could snap his fingers, Zara stopped him. 'Don't put the lights back on,' she warned. 'They might still have someone watching the house.'

'What if there's someone watching the front?' said Sam. 'Is it safe to go out?'

Zara hesitated. The three of them stood in the centre of the room, barely able to see each other. In just a few terrible minutes, all the warmth and light had been sucked out of their home, leaving it a cold, dark place of danger. What should they do?

'Why didn't the professors hide too?' asked Ben in a hollow voice.

'Because then the men would have searched the house

and found us three as well,' said Zara. 'Come on, I think we'll have to risk using the front d–'

'COME OOT OF THERE!'

The three children leapt with fright as a man's voice burst in from the French windows. A beam of torch light pierced through the room. Sam flung himself under the table, falling on top of Ben, bracing himself for a blast of gunfire. But as the man continued shouting, Sam realized it wasn't one of the gunmen. It was Mr Skinner.

'I saw ye, Ampersand!' ranted their neighbour from the doorway. 'Crashin' roond yer garden in some crackpot flying machine! I ken ye've damaged ma property 'cos ma phone's gone deid! I'll huv ye fer this! Come oot! I ken ye're in there!'

'Mr Skinner, our uncle's not here!' interrupted Zara, emerging from behind a chair. 'He's been kidnapped! And the others! In that plane you saw! We've got to phone the police!'

'Kidnapped!' exclaimed Mr Skinner. 'Ye expect me tae believe yer stupid kid's stories? I ken whit's happened.' His torch beam flashed across the half-eaten meal, the glasses and wine bottles, the broken glass around the shattered French windows. 'He got drunk, didn't he? With all those drop-oot pals o' his who've bin arriving at all hoors today. They've smashed the place up and noo they're away joy-riding in that machine and . . .' His torch beam settled on the faces of the three children. 'Wait a minute!' he cried. 'He's left youse all alone! *And ye're no' auld enough tae be left!*' His eyes glinted in triumph. 'He's done it noo! He's broken the law! Gone off drunk an' left youse alone in this mess! Ye'll be taken intae care! I'm going up tae the phone box tae call the police! They'll huv tae listen tae me noo!'

'No!' shouted Ben. 'You've got it all wrong! We're telling the truth!'

But Mr Skinner, cackling with delight, had disappeared out into the foggy garden and back across to his house.

'Come on!' said Ben, rushing to the front door, 'We've got to phone the police before he does.'

'No!' shouted Zara. Ben and Sam looked at her, confused. 'Don't you see?' she went on. 'The police won't believe us any more than Mr Skinner did! That plane won't show up on any radar screens. Mr Skinner will tell them all sorts of lies about Uncle Alexander and they'll waste days and days questioning us and by the time we persuade them to even think about organizing a search of Nordbergen, it'll be too late – Uncle Alexander and the others will be dead! They've only got till Wednesday and it's Sunday night now!'

'But what else *can* we do?' asked Ben desperately.

'*I don't know!*' wailed Zara. She held her brother's hand and they stood in silence, frozen by the hopelessness of it all.

'Hang on!' said Sam, suddenly recalling something. 'Professor Gauntraker *said* there'd be no point in going to the police. He knew we were listening. And that was when he dropped the button!'

'What button?' asked Ben.

'His jacket cuff button. I'm sure he knew where I was hiding; knew I could see what he was doing. He broke off the button and let it drop to the floor.'

'The secret instructions!' exclaimed Zara. 'He was telling us to use the secret way of getting to Nordbergen, to rescue them!' She rushed to a work bench, rummaged around the pile of junk and pulled out a rusty old bike lamp. 'Me and Sam'll find the button. Ben, you go upstairs and stuff some warm clothes and our torches and anything else you think'll be useful into our rucksacks. Bring Sam's too and bring all the money there is in our money boxes. But hurry, before Mr Skinner brings the police!'

On their hands and knees, by the dim light of the bike lamp, Sam and Zara frantically scanned the none-too-tidy floor between the table and the staircase. 'But we can't just head off to the Arctic!' protested Sam. 'Even if there *is* some secret way of getting someone to take us there, it's too far. We should phone my mum and dad.'

'All right,' conceded Zara. 'You can phone your parents as soon as we get safely away from here. If they can help us, fine. But if they can't, Ben and I are going to Nordbergen, however we have to get there. We've got to do everything we can to try and rescue Uncle Alexander and the others before they're murdered.'

Suddenly Sam caught sight of something small and round beneath a clump of trailing ivy. 'Found it!' he exclaimed, pouncing on the button. It looked like an ordinary old-fashioned button, made of deer horn.

'Well done!' said Zara. 'We'll look at it properly after we've phoned your parents. Here's Ben with the rucksacks. Let's get our coats on and go.'

Chapter Twelve

Quietly and cautiously, Zara, Ben and Sam slipped out through the front door of 12 Pinkerton Place. They headed downhill, away from the phone box which Mr Skinner would be using, and walked towards the city centre. They kept a sharp look out for any  approaching police cars, though the dense fog considerably lessened the chances of anyone spotting them.

Zara and Ben knew their way around these streets well and after walking briskly for half a mile or so, they reached a secluded square of stone tenements with a phone box at one corner.

As Sam had expected, his Great-Aunt Roberta answered the phone. 'This is Sam,' he said. 'Are Mum or Dad there?'

'They're out at that conference of theirs,' Great-Aunt Roberta informed him, rather sharply. 'Some sort of fancy-dress disco apparently. At their age! They went out looking perfectly *ridiculous* dressed as two tins of peas.'

Sam's heart sank. Whilst he knew that his parents would have grasped the situation immediately and known what to do for the best, he wasn't so sure about Great Aunt Roberta. 'Why are you ringing, Sam?' she continued suspiciously. 'Are you in trouble? I *said* it was highly irresponsible, letting a boy of your age go off to a foreign country like Scotland with some college professor we hardly know. Something's gone wrong, hasn't it?'

'No, no!' said Sam, hurriedly. 'Everything's fine. I was just ringing to say hi. I'll try again tomorrow. Bye.' He quickly replaced the receiver, wishing that his parents were not quite so against mobile phones.

'You did the right thing,' Zara reassured Sam when he reported the conversation. 'Now let's have a look at that button.'

The three of them crowded into the phone box and Sam placed the button on the metal shelf. A quick examination of its front and back revealed nothing unusual.

'It must open up,' guessed Ben. 'See, there's a thin crack round the rim, where the two halves join.'

Sam took his Swiss army knife from his rucksack pocket and slid the thinnest blade into the crack. He twisted the knife carefully and prised the two halves of the button apart. A tiny disc of white paper was pasted onto the inside of the back half.

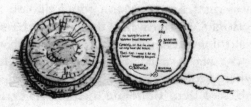

'There's some sort of marks on it,' said Zara, holding it up to her eyes, 'but no one could read writing that small.'

'Hang on,' said Sam. 'I've got a magnifying glass on my clock-compass.' Through Sam's magnifying glass they could all make out several words and a diagram, still tiny but now legible.

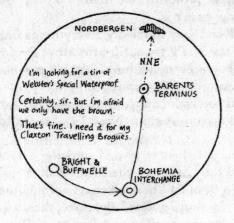

'I'll write it out bigger,' said Sam. He fished out his notebook and a pen and made an enlarged copy.

'That bit about Webster's Special Waterproof and stuff doesn't make any sense,' said Ben. 'But the diagram could be some sort of map.'

'Yeah!' agreed Zara. 'Maybe your idea about secret airfields was right, Sam. See, you could take off from a place called Bright & Buffwelle, then you'd have to change flights at somewhere called Bohemia Interchange, then fly north to a place called Barents Terminus. That could be near where Professor Murdo left them stranded.'

'Yeah,' said Ben. 'Bohemia Interchange could be in the Czech Republic.'

'But where's Bright & Buffwelle?' asked Sam. 'I've never heard of a place called that.'

'Wait,' said Zara. 'I know the name from somewhere.' She screwed her face up in fierce concentration. 'It's a shop,' she remembered suddenly. 'A shop in St Stephen Street. I've never been in but we've passed it sometimes. I think it sells shoe polish.'

'But there can't be an airfield in a shop!' Ben pointed out.

'Well . . . *I* don't know,' admitted Zara. 'Maybe it's a secret travel agents or something. The shop'll be closed at this time of night but there might be someone there who knows how to help us. Come on, we have to try it. We have to try *anything*.' Gathering up the button and their rucksacks, they strode onwards, Zara setting a demanding pace.

The brightly lit city centre that Sam remembered from two nights ago had been transformed by the fog into a ghostly, mysterious place. The haar drifted relentlessly out of the wide Georgian side streets and onto Princes Street in huge, pale grey fingers. Shadowy fragments of spires and statues slipped in and out of visibility through the rolling shroud of mist. The castle itself had all but vanished into the grey void of Princes Street Gardens.

At the junction with Frederick Street, Zara stopped. 'Look, Sam,' she said. 'If you think you ought to wait somewhere safe and try to phone your mum and dad again later, then maybe you should. It's different for me and Ben. We've got no one else. We've got nothing to lose. But we shouldn't drag you off to somewhere that might be dangerous when you haven't told your parents.'

Sam thought about this, but not for long. 'No,' he said. 'I'll stick with you two. Mum and Dad wouldn't want me to leave you now.'

'Thanks,' said Zara. From Zara and Ben's looks of relief, Sam knew he'd made the right decision.

They strode purposefully along Frederick Street and on down Howe Street.

'Isn't it a bit odd having a shop that only sells shoe polish?' asked Sam.

Zara shrugged. 'Edinburgh's full of peculiar shops like that,' she said. 'There's a shop on Victoria Street that sells nothing but brushes.'

They reached the foot of the long hill. The massive clock tower of St Stephen's Church loomed above them through the fog. 'It's gone eleven,' observed Ben as they passed beneath the church steps and followed the cobbled road round into St Stephen Street. 'I hope we don't have to wake anyone up.'

But, to their surprise, Bright & Buffwelle appeared to be open. Warm yellow light glowed through the square windowpanes of the small red shop, which was situated halfway along the street. The three children peered in. The walls were lined with shelves stacked high with flat circular tins. Behind a wood-panelled counter sat a round-faced, grey-haired man in a dark green pullover, reading a newspaper.

'Well, if we don't go in and ask, we'll never find out anything,' said Zara, with more confidence than she felt. A bell pinged gently as she opened the door and led them into the shop. The shopkeeper looked up from his paper. 'Can I help you?' he asked politely. The delicious smell of shoe polish, which pervaded the cosy atmosphere of the shop, somehow made the children feel a little less nervous.

58

'Well ... er ... we hope so,' began Zara hesitantly. 'You see ... er ... someone we know sort of told us that you might be able to ... er ... help us get to a place called Barents Terminus. It's ... um ... in the Arctic,' she added feeling more foolish by the second. 'We need to get to Nordbergen.'

'I'm afraid I haven't got the faintest idea what you're talking about,' said the man, still politely, but firmly. 'This is a shoe polish shop. We sell shoe polish.'

'Oh,' said Zara. 'Sorry. Our mistake.' Of course it was just a shop. Why had she allowed herself to hope it might be anything else? Because it had been their only real hope. She was close to tears as they turned to leave.

'Wait!' said Ben, tugging at Sam's sleeve. Ben looked straight at the shopkeeper and said: 'I'm looking for a tin of Webster's Special Waterproof.'

For a second, Sam and Zara stared at Ben as if he'd gone mad. Then a look of understanding came into their eyes and they watched the shopkeeper intently, waiting with baited breath for him to speak.

'Certainly, sir,' he replied, his face giving nothing away. 'But I'm afraid we only have the brown.'

Sam felt a tingle rise up the skin of his face. 'That's fine,' Ben recited, carefully recalling the exact words. 'I need it for my Claxton Travelling Brogues.'

In absolute silence, the man pressed a button on the side of his shop till. It slid a little way along the counter and another, bulkier-looking till rose up from a concealed compartment to take its place. 'That's better,' said the man. 'Sorry to have appeared unhelpful but you should have used the password straight away. We can't be too careful, as you know.'

'Yeah, sorry, we sort of forgot,' said Zara, shooting the boys a warning glance. The man clearly assumed that they knew a great deal more about this secret than they actually did. If they admitted that they knew nothing, he might not help them at all.

'No harm done,' said the man, pleasantly. 'Now then, three tickets to Barents Terminus, was it?' He punched some buttons on the till's keyboard and checked a small screen. 'That'll be thirty-six pounds sixty please.' The till clicked and whirred.

Zara handed over four ten-pound notes from her purse. They didn't have much money between them but if Barents Terminus was as far away as they thought it was, then a fare of twelve pounds twenty each was remarkably good value.

The man caught the tickets as they flew out of a slot in the side of the till and handed one to each of them. 'You'll just catch the 23:30 eastbound service,' he said. 'Change at Bohemia Interchange onto the Far Northern. Have a good trip.'

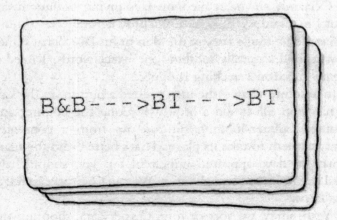

The three children stood there awkwardly. Where were they supposed to go now? The airport? Waverley Station? The Bus Station? The tickets themselves – three identical rectangles of manilla card with a simple line of text printed on one side and a magnetic strip on the other – offered no further clues.

'Downstairs.' The man smiled, indicating a small wooden stairway at the back of the shop. 'The Hardie's Invincible Scuff-Proof.'

Trying not to look as mystified as they felt, Sam, Ben and Zara made their way down into the basement, a window-less room much smaller than the upstairs shop. Fitted shelves along one wall were filled, like the shelves upstairs, with neatly stacked tins of shoe polish. There seemed to be hundreds of different makes – Captain's Extra-Gleam Boot Black, MacBurnish's Patent Weatherguard, Wainwright's 'Famous Fell Beater' Dubbin.

'It's going to take ages to find this Hardie's Invincible whatever-it-was,' said Sam.

'No, it's all right – they're stacked alphabetically,' noticed Zara. Even so, it took them a couple of minutes to find the small, solitary tin of Hardie's Invincible Scuff-Proof, hiding at the back of a shelf between several tins of Glossmore Original Deep Shine and a stack of Hunter's Guaranteed Seam Wax.

'It's stuck to the shelf!' discovered Zara, attempting to pick the tin up.

'Let me try,' said Ben but he couldn't move it either.

'Will it open?' asked Sam, reaching for the lid.

At first Sam tried, in vain, to pull the lid off with his fingertips. Then he noticed that, like most shoe polish tins, the lid had a section at one side marked PRESS TO OPEN. The side of the lid shifted down beneath his thumb, with a tinny clunk. Then, suddenly, everything around them seemed to spin.

A second later, the movement stopped. They were still facing the same section of shelving but, looking round, they found themselves to be in a different, even tinier space – a two-metre square, wood-panelled box room with a red door in the wall opposite them.

'This bit of floor must have spun round 180 degrees!' exclaimed Sam, pointing down to the visible half of the flat disc they were standing on. 'This shelf is a secret rotating door!'

'You're right,' agreed Zara. 'But what's through this red door?'

They stepped forward and, as their feet left the disc, it rotated back again, closing them in with another wood-panelled wall.

Ben peered through the red door's little diamond-shaped window. 'Looks like a lift,' he said. He slid the door sideways and the three children stepped into the small, linoleum-lined chamber. The lift smelled pleasantly of beeswax and machine oil and was warmly lit by a rose-coloured glass lantern in the ceiling. There were no buttons inside but, as the door trundled shut behind them, they heard a soft click followed by a low, constant hum. With a gentle jolt, the lift began to descend.

Chapter Thirteen

The lift rumbled steadily downwards. Sam, Zara and Ben stared through the little window, which cast a diamond-shaped patch of light onto the endlessly rising lift-shaft wall.

'Where are we going?' asked Zara, breaking the silence after several minutes. 'There can't be another cellar *this* far down.'

'I've never been in a lift that went down for this long,' said Sam. 'Not even on the London Underground.'

'*An underground!*' exclaimed Ben. 'That's where this lift is taking us — *to a secret underground railway!*'

'Don't be silly!' said Zara. 'There *can't* be an underground railway all the way to the Arctic. That would be impossible.'

'It *sounds* impossible,' conceded Ben. 'But if it *did* exist, it *would* count as one of the most extraordinary secrets in the world.'

Before Zara or Sam could reply, a dimly lit room ascended into view outside and the lift landed with a gentle bump. Automatically, the door slid open and the three children stepped out.

The room was no bigger than the one from which they had just descended. Its walls and arched ceiling were covered in red and cream tiles. A narrow gap in the wall in front of them led into a tiled passage which curved round out of sight but their way through was blocked by the black metal bars of a pair of turnstile gates.

Zara pushed at the gates but nothing would make them turn. 'The bars are too close together to climb through,' she said. 'There must be another secret button or something.' However, a thorough investigation of the gates revealed nothing.

'What about this?' said Sam suddenly. He'd noticed a small brass plaque with a horizontal slot in it, set into the tiles to the side of the right-hand gateway. 'Maybe we're supposed to put our tickets into it.'

'Of course,' said Zara. She slid her ticket into the slot and pushed again at the turnstile, which rotated to let her through. She retrieved her ticket from an identical slot on the other side and quickly passed the other two tickets back to the boys, who followed her.

After a short distance, the curving passage brought them onto a narrow platform. The platform ran along one side of a long tube-shaped space, again lined with cream and red tiles. Each end of the space led off into a dark tunnel. Red enamel signs, fixed at regular intervals along the walls, carried the name

in white capital letters.

There could be no doubt now that Ben's guess had been correct; they were clearly standing on the platform of some sort of underground railway station.

'The tunnel's a bit smaller than the ones on any underground I've been on,' observed Zara.

'There aren't any tracks down on the bottom of the tunnel,' noticed Ben, looking over the edge of the platform.

'But there's a sort of metal rail, look, running along the ceiling,' pointed out Sam. 'What kind of vehicle could run on that?'

'We'll soon find out,' said Zara. 'Listen.'

From the tunnel to their left came a distant sound, barely audible at first but steadily growing in volume. It was the sound of rushing wind, accompanied by a rhythmic *clickety-click . . . clickety-click . . .* Huddled together, they peered into the darkness, seeing nothing. Then, 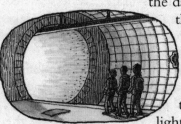 they could just make out a faint glow, hardly permeating the inky blackness; then a flickering gleam, spilling round a distant curve in the tunnel; then a single spot of light, growing as it sped towards them. The rush of wind rose to a roar, the clickety-click crescendoed to a clatter and, finally, the mysterious subterranean train hurtled out of the shadows. Instinctively Zara clutched the boys' arms and pulled them back from the edge of the platform.

The train consisted of three metallic grey bullet-shaped sections, each one only six metres long and two metres high. There were no wheels beneath. Instead, the whole train was suspended from the metal rail on the ceiling of the tunnel by a series of metal arms positioned along the top of the train, two to each section. Each arm was connected to the rail with a wheeled trolley mechanism. The front section of the train, clearly the engine, had no windows other than those of the streamlined driver's cab, which looked forward over the single round headlamp. Behind the cab, a complex arrangement of panels, hatches and grilles had been built into the heavily riveted bodywork. The children caught only a fleeting glimpse of two drivers as the engine rolled past and the train braked to a standstill beside them.

The two carriages behind the engine each had five brass porthole windows down either side. The middle portholes were set into the carriage doors, which now slid open with a hiss. From the rear carriage, a serious-looking man wearing a black raincoat and beret stepped out onto the platform. He raised his beret politely to the children as he scurried away down the passage without a word, presumably to take the lift up to the surface. He had been the only passenger; both carriages were now empty.

'Come on,' said Zara and the three of them stepped into the first carriage. The door hissed shut and the train moved forward once more.

They sat down near the middle of the carriage on the comfortable red leather seating which ran down each side of the cylindrical interior. Zara sat facing Sam and Ben, their rucksacks on the seats next to them. The carriage was warm and well lit by rows of small light bulbs set into the ceiling. By the light cast through the portholes, they could see the walls of the tunnel rumbling past. The tunnel was rougher and rockier than the tunnels Sam remembered from travelling on the London Underground, though as the train picked up speed the stony walls became just a grey blur flashing past.

'It feels a bit strange not being able to see where we are and where we're going,' said Zara. 'There's not even a map on the wall.'

Sam took his clock-compass out of his rucksack. 'We're heading more or less south at the moment,' he said.

Ben brought his own brass compass out of his rucksack and a folded-up map of the world, which he partially unfolded to show Western Europe. 'It's hard to plot our course when we don't know how fast we're going,' he said.

'Where did you say you thought Bohemia Interchange

might be, Ben?' asked Zara. 'In the Czech Republic?'

Ben nodded. 'I'm sure Bohemia's an old name for somewhere round there,' he explained. 'If we *are* going that far, it's going to take a while even if we're going *really* fast. And we've still got to get from there to this Barents Terminus place.'

'Even if we *can* get all the way to Barents Terminus, how do we get to Nordbergen from there?' wondered Sam. He studied the diagram he'd copied into his notebook. 'I reckon it says that Nordbergen is north-north-east of Barents Terminus – look – but it doesn't say how far.'

'My map's not much help,' said Ben. 'Too small a scale. It doesn't even have Nordbergen on it.'

'If Barents Terminus is near to where Professor Murdo dumped them all on the ice, it must be hundreds of miles from anywhere,' said Zara. 'They were flying for an hour, locked in the cargo hold, remember.'

'If we *do* get to Nordbergen, how are we going to rescue your uncle and the others?' asked Sam.

'Should we ask the people who run this underground system for help?' asked Ben. 'Do you think they know Professor Gauntraker? Would they help us or would they say we shouldn't be using their secret underground and send us back?'

'*I* don't know!' said Zara. She looked across at Ben and Sam's tired, worried faces, seeing more unanswerable questions forming in their minds. This wasn't good. If they carried on like this they'd find themselves asking whether Uncle Alexander was still alive. She forced herself to speak more cheerfully. 'Look, we can work out what to do and who to ask for help as we go,' she said. 'We've done pretty well so far. We worked out Professor Gauntraker's secret instructions, we found this underground railway and we're well on our way. It'll be all right.'

Sam *had* been about to ask where they were going to get food from – it seemed a very long time since their last meal at Professor Ampersand's house had been so violently interrupted – but he stopped himself. He realized that Zara, who must be as hungry and tired as himself, was making a huge effort to be optimistic and he resolved not to worry about things out loud any more. 'Zara's right,' he said. 'We're doing what Professor Gauntraker thought we should do and it'll work out in the end.'

'Yeah,' said Ben, hugely reassured by his older sister's confidence and proud that Sam trusted her too. 'It'll be fine. Hey!' he added, suddenly remembering something. 'Anyone want some chocolate? I packed the Easter egg I'd bought for you into my rucksack with my clothes.'

'Ben,' said Zara, 'you're a genius.'

'You can't go travelling without chocolate.' Ben grinned. 'Pity I didn't know you were coming to stay when I bought it, Sam. Otherwise we'd have two.'

They carefully unwrapped the chocolate egg and split it into quarters. 'We'll have a quarter each,' suggested Zara, 'and save the last bit to share later, in case we really need it.'

They munched their chocolate ravenously and, whilst nobody felt exactly full once the three pieces were gone, they all felt considerably happier inside.

Sam remembered something else. He took out all the money he had brought with him for the week – thirty pounds – and handed it to Zara. 'Here, Zara. You paid for my ticket,' he said. 'We should pool all our money together anyway. You keep it, with yours and Ben's.'

'Well, all right,' agreed Zara. 'But I'll pay you back seventeen pounds eighty if we don't need to spend any more.'

The carriage tilted and swung as the train hurtled round the bends of the tunnel. However, Ben found it was possible to stand up and move around if you didn't mind occasionally being flung down onto a seat. He made his way gingerly along to the rear of the carriage to inspect a windowless door in the end wall. 'I want to see if this leads across to the next carriage,' he said.

'Ben, don't!' cried Zara. 'You might fall out!'

But she needn't have worried. 'It's all right. It doesn't lead out of the carriage at all,' Ben reported. 'It's a toilet.'

'Thank goodness for that!' said Zara, leaping up from her seat. 'I'm bursting.'

Several minutes later, after they had all availed themselves of the impressively hi-tech toilet facilities and returned to their seats, the constant *clickety-click* from the wheels on the rail above them began to change.

'We're slowing down!' said Sam.

'D'you think this can be Bohemia Interchange already?' asked Ben.

'Dunno,' said Zara. 'But we've arrived somewhere.'

Chapter Fourteen

Sam, Ben and Zara peered out of the portholes as their carriage emerged into a station which was very similar to Bright & Buffwelle, except that the tiles surrounding this platform were green and cream. The signs along the walls read

OBBLETHWAITE MILL

'There must be other stops along the line before we get to Bohemia Interchange,' said Sam.

'Unless we got on the wrong train,' worried Zara. 'Did anyone actually notice if it was 11.30 when we got on?'

'We could ask one of these other passengers,' suggested Ben, looking out of the windows as the train trundled sedately to a standstill beside a group of seven people waiting on the platform.

A young couple carrying parcels, two men carrying a violin case and a guitar case, and a grey-haired man in a grey suit got into the carriage behind them. A neatly dressed elderly lady in a felt hat and a man in a brown coat, who didn't seem to be together, got into their carriage. The man nodded politely as he passed the children on his way to a seat at one end of the carriage. He sat down, leaned back with his eyes shut and began to snore. The elderly lady ignored them completely, sat down at the other end of the carriage and buried herself in a book.

The door hissed and was just sliding shut when the children saw another man rushing out of a tiled passageway and onto the platform. 'Wait!' he shouted. The door reopened and the man leapt into the carriage calling 'Ta!' to the drivers as he did so. He flopped down, panting, on the seat next to Ben's rucksack, as the door closed and the train began to move again. He was a rather dishevelled man in his mid-forties wearing faded jeans, battered trainers and a crumpled corduroy jacket (which was slightly too small for him) over a white T-shirt. He clutched a small shoulder bag with a broken zip, from which a sock and a tube of toothpaste were trying to escape. He had dark curly hair, long over his neck and ears, though beginning to thin on the top of his head. A grin spread over his weather-beaten tanned face. 'Phew!' he said to the children. 'I was cutting that a bit fine, wasn't I?'

From her seat at the end of the carriage, the elderly lady frowned at the man from over her book, clearly not approving of people who cut things a bit fine, nor of people who talked in railway carriages.

'Evening, madam,' said the man loudly, tipping the lady a friendly wink, which caused her to scowl and retreat back into her book. He turned back to the children. 'Sorry,' he said. 'Were you kids trying to get some kip?'

'No, it's all right,' replied Zara. 'This *is* the right train for Bohemia Interchange, isn't it?'

''Course,' said the man. 'All services on the Western European Line run all the way from Mowdie End to Bohemia Interchange. And back again, of course. Long as you get on a train going in the right direction, you can't go wrong. First journey on the ISNT, is it?'

'Er . . . on the what?' asked Zara. What did he mean, 'on the isn't is it'?

'The ISNT!' repeated the man. 'The Intercontinental Subterranean Navigation & Transportation Company.'

'Oh. Is that what this is called?' said Zara.

The man peered at them curiously. 'You didn't even know *that*?' he asked.

'Well . . . er . . . we . . .' stumbled Zara, silently cursing herself for revealing their ignorance.

'We were sort of shown how to travel this way by someone,' chipped in Ben. 'It was an emergency. There wasn't time to explain much to us. But we're supposed to be here, honest.'

'Oh, don't look so worried,' smiled the man. 'I ain't prying. I'm the last person to pry into the business of other passengers. But . . . er . . . best keep our voices down a bit, eh?' He flashed a glance towards the lady. 'Some members can be a bit particular about the credentials of their fellow travellers. Nah then,' he continued, 'if you want to know more about the ISNT, you're asking the right person. Me name's Jack, by the way. Jack Dodgenham. I've travelled every mile of the entire network. Made it me lifetime's study.'

'I'm Zara,' said Zara, 'and this is my brother Ben and our friend Sam.'

'Pleased to make yer acquaintances,' said Jack, shaking their hands in turn. Then he reached into a jacket pocket and brought out a creased and battered red paperback booklet. 'These ISNT atlases are pretty hard to get hold of,' he told them. 'The Board of Directors has always worried that printed maps might jeopardize the secrecy of the system in the outside world, like, so they don't print many.' He opened the booklet's yellowing pages and showed the children a map.

'See, we're travelling along this line here, The Western European. It goes down into Belgium, France, across Germany and finishes up at Bohemia Interchange in Czechoslovakia – no, I mean the Czech Republic these days, don't I? From there you can get onto three other lines: the Southern Express, the Far Northern and the

Grand Orient. I'm going along the Grand Orient meself, to Istanbul. See me kids.'

'But there must be *thousands* of miles of tunnels!' exclaimed Sam. 'How did they all get built?'

'Ah,' said Jack. 'That's a very good point. You'd think that it would be virtually impossible to construct that many miles of tunnel, wouldn't you? And you'd be dead right. The truth is, the vast majority of the tunnels that make up the ISNT network ain't man-made at all; they're natural cave systems carved out of the rock by underground rivers over thousands, maybe millions of years.

'It was a French bloke who founded the ISNT. A shy, short-sighted geologist by the name of Jean-Pierre Taupe. He started exploring caves in the 1870s, studying fossils and whatnot. Soon became obsessed with the caves themselves. Somehow felt at home down there. He began to go further underground than anyone had ever gone before, making expeditions all over Europe, discovering networks of caves far more extensive than anything known about at the time. Or known about by most people now, come to that. By meticulous navigation, Jean-Pierre eventually deduced that many of these cave systems ended only a few miles from where others began, and could be linked by sections of man-made tunnelling. For instance, he was sure that two tunnels he'd discovered going deep under the English Channel, one from each side, passed close enough to each other to be joined up.

'Well, in 1892 he decided to share his discoveries with two other people: a Scottish engineer called Hector Henderson, who'd made a name for himself building railway tunnels; and a German bird called Countess Clara von Maulwurf who was a bit of an inventor. She was obsessed by the possibilities of electrical power and most people then thought she was bonkers. But Jean-Pierre had a bit of a soft spot for her. Also, being a countess, she was loaded, which came in handy. Together, they founded the Intercontinental Subterranean Navigation & Transportation Company.

'The first decision they made was that the whole thing had to be kept secret. They worried that any government who got to hear about these tunnels might want to use 'em for warlike purposes, whereas *their* vision was to create a high-speed travel system to increase international under-standing. Yer actual World Wide Web of its time, like. Its members were to be approved by the board and sworn to secrecy.

'Well, they went at it hammer and tongs, recruiting engineers, architects and labourers, who all became members of the project and were sworn to secrecy. They bored out new tunnels, widened caves, pumped out water, fixed the overhead rail along the whole route and built the under-ground stations. Difficult, dangerous work; by far the most ambitious engineering project of the age, and all done in secret.

'Countess von Maulwurf herself designed the electric trains. They were built in some of the bigger caves along the route, which are still used as maintenance workshops today. Because there's only one tunnel, trains go back and forth along the same rail. At some of the bigger stations, the rail splits into two, one going each side of the platform so that the trains can pass each other safely. Wouldn't want two trains meeting head-on in a tunnel, would you?'

'No, you wouldn't!' agreed Zara, looking a bit worried by the thought.

'It's all right.' Jack grinned. 'There ain't never been a crash on the ISNT. Anyway, by January the first, 1900, the line we're travelling along now was complete and the first train made its maiden voyage from Oban, on the West of Scotland – see, that's Mowdie End on the map – to Bohemia Interchange. You can just imagine it, can't you? Old Jean-Pierre and the Countess up there in the driver's cab, Hector back here, knocking back the bubbly with the workers. Wish I'd been there.

'Once they'd got the Western European line up and running, there was no stopping 'em. They took on yet more workers and started on the other lines. By 1936, the network as we know it today was more or less complete. Jean-Pierre Taupe lived to see his vision fulfilled, dying in 1937.'

'It's amazing!' said Sam. 'I can't believe this has all been kept secret for so long.'

'The thing about the ISNT,' observed Jack, 'is that it sounds so unbelievable that anyone who does get to hear about it doesn't believe it. Unless they see it with their own eyes, and then they love the idea of travelling on it so much that they become members and don't tell no one else. Phew! That's a lot of talking,' Jack concluded, pulling a bottle of water from his bag. 'You kids want a drink?'

It was warm inside the little carriage and they each accepted a sip before Jack put the bottle to his lips and glugged down half the contents. 'Ah, that's better!' he said, wiping his mouth with the back of his hand. 'Wish I'd brought some chocolate, though. I could just do with a bit of chocolate, couldn't you?'

Zara glanced at the boys, who nodded. 'We've got some chocolate left,' she said. 'D'you want it?'

'Aw, no, I don't wanna take yer food off you,' Jack said, as Zara handed him the remaining bit of Easter egg. 'Oh, well, go on then, if you're sure you've had enough. Tell you what, I'll buy you all breakfast when we get to Bohemia Interchange. That's a promise.'

'How long will it take us to get there?' asked Zara.

'Oh, a long time yet,' said Jack. 'We'll be stopping at North Downs soon; that's the last stop before we go under the Channel, like. Then it's another five and a half hours to Bohemia Interchange. Not bad going when you remember it's over eight hundred miles away.'

Ben yawned and Zara suddenly realized how tired they all were. They'd been up since six in the morning, and now it was nearly half-past one the following morning. 'You boys should get some sleep,' she said.

'We all should,' said Ben.

'I suppose so,' said Zara hesitantly. She knew she'd have to sleep at some point but shouldn't one of them stay awake to guard their bags? And what if they didn't wake up when they got to Bohemia Interchange?

'It's all right,' said Jack. 'I'll keep an eye on yer stuff and wake you just before we get there.'

'Thanks,' said Zara. She took her coat off and laid it over herself, lying over a couple of seats. The boys followed her example and, within two minutes of wishing each other goodnight, all three of them were sleeping soundly.

Chapter Fifteen

'Marcia.'

'Uh? . . . Where am I?'

'It's all right, Marcia darling . . . You're in your bed, at home, of course.'

'Feel . . . funny . . . Can't . . . wake . . . up . . .'

'You don't have to wake up, darling . . . Just sit up and let me put your coat on over your pyjamas . . . That's it.'

'What? . . . What for? . . . What time is it?'

'It's the middle of the night . . . Don't wake up . . . Let Daddy carry you . . . That's it . . . You can sleep in the car.'

'Uh? . . . Why are we going in the car? . . . Where are we going? . . .'

'Just a little trip, darling . . . We'll be there in the morning.'

'No . . . Wanna stay in bed . . . Feel funny . . .'

'Drink this, darling . . . That's it . . . that's it . . . Go back to sleep . . .'

In the car . . . Where are we going? . . . Still dark . . . Want to sit up . . . see out . . . No . . . Too tired . . . Can't move . . . Too tired . . . Sleeping again . . . Sleep . . .

Cold . . . Car door open . . . Car stopped . . . Where are we? . . .

'Ssh, darling . . . Don't wake up . . . Let Daddy carry you again . . . That's it . . . Ssh . . .'

Can't open eyes . . . Must open eyes . . . Trees . . . grass . . . All dark . . . Must be in a field . . . What's that? . . . A plane . . . Why are we going on a plane? . . . Don't want to go on the plane . . . Don't want to go on the plane . . .

'Don't want to go on the plane!'

'Ssh, darling . . . Calm down . . . Drink some more water . . . That's it . . .'

A bird's head . . . on the plane . . . on the tail . . . A black bird . . . Crow or something . . . We're getting into the plane . . .

'That's it, darling . . . Lie down here and go back to sleep . . . We'll be there in the morning.'

'Where? . . . Where are we going? . . . Don't . . . feel . . . right . . .'

'Don't worry . . . We're just going on a little trip . . . We're taking you somewhere to make you better.'

Chapter Sixteen

Ben opened his eyes, realizing that the train had stopped. He had been vaguely aware of stopping at a couple of stations during the night but wasn't sure how many other stops he'd slept through completely. They couldn't be at Bohemia Interchange already could they? Jack had promised to wake them. He looked up at the seat next to them. Jack was fast asleep, head lolled back and mouth wide open. However, the elderly lady, the man in the suit and several other passengers (who must have boarded en route) were gathering up their belongings and disembarking. Ben sat up suddenly. Sure enough, the signs along the tiled walls read

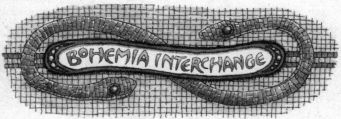

'Zara, Sam, wake up! We're here!' he exclaimed, giving Sam a shake. Sam and Zara sat up, blinking blearily.

'Are you sure?' Zara yawned.

'Uh! . . . Eh? . . . Whassup?' snuffled Jack, jerking himself upright. 'We here already? Must've nodded off meself . . . just for a minute, like.' He stood up, slapped his cheeks with both hands and swept his fingers back through his long hair. 'Come on then,' he said, swinging his bag over his shoulder. 'Let's go into the Central Hall and see about getting ourselves some breakfast.'

The platform chamber was wide and circular, with the overhead rail forming a large loop so that the train would be able to trundle round and return through the tunnel. The turnstile platform gates were more ornate than at Bright & Buffwelle, their bronze bars cast into elegant twists and curls. Their decorative style was matched in the swirling, colourful designs of the wall tiles.

'Art Nouveau, this style's known as,' said Jack knowledgeably, noticing the children gazing around them. 'One of the most beautiful stations on the whole network, this is. Oh, drat! These bloomin' machines.' The slot beside the turnstile had spat his ticket back out and the gate wouldn't turn. He tried again and this time the turnstile let him pass. The children went through without incident and followed Jack along a winding passageway. The platform's pleasant smell of oiled machinery and electric motors gave way to the delicious aroma of food being cooked. Also emanating from somewhere ahead was the sound of human activity: the hubbub of echoing voices, the clatter of cutlery and the click-clack of footsteps pacing across a marble floor. The noise crescendoed to a clamouring din as they emerged into the vast Central Hall of Bohemia Interchange.

The hall had clearly once been an enormous natural cave and the fabulous Art Nouveau decor perfectly suited the undulating curves of the walls and ceiling. Opulent mosaics seemed to flow over every inch of rock. Bronze serpents twisted out of the walls supporting spherical frosted-glass lanterns between their teeth. As well as their entrance, three other large passageways led into the hall. Above each of these four portals, multi-lingual signs proclaimed the names of the different underground lines:

THE WESTERN EUROPEAN

THE SOUTHERN EXPRESS

THE GRAND ORIENT

THE FAR NORTHERN

People of every description criss-crossed the hall, bustling in and out of the ticket offices and cafés that had been built into alcoves around the central space: people garbed in every variety of clothing – heavy overcoats with fur hats, bright saris, rugged safari suits, formal dinner jackets, flowing robes and burkas; people greeting and parting, whispering and shouting, joking and arguing in every imaginable language.

Sam spotted the two musicians who had been on their train. They were warmly greeting three old men who were emerging from the Grand Orient passageway, dressed in magnificent silken jackets and fur-trimmed hats, and carrying strange multi-stringed musical instruments.

'We ought to see when the next Far Northern train leaves,' said Zara anxiously. 'Make sure we've got time to have breakfast here.'

'Going up the Far Northern, are you?' said Jack. 'Well, we can easily check.' He led them over to the entrance of the Far Northern passageway, beside which a wooden board informed them:

'We've got ages then,' said Zara, looking at her watch as they headed over to an alcove café. 'It's only five past seven.'

'You're forgetting we've travelled a time-zone east-ward,' Jack pointed out. 'See, it's five past eight here.' He pointed to a large four-faced clock positioned on top of a squat round tower in the centre of the hall.

They sat down on stools around one of the high tables beside the café. 'Now, I'd recommend their Special International Breakfast,' said Jack. 'Porridge, grilled fish, bacon and eggs, bratwurst, dumplings, kedgeree, ham, cheese, croissants, churros, pomegranates, mangoes, banana fritters, coffee, hot chocolate, coconut milk, yak butter tea, the lot.'

'We *should* have a good breakfast, whilst we've got the chance,' said Ben.

'That's my motto in life,' said Jack turning to the approaching waiter. 'Four Specials, son,' he said, speaking extra loudly and holding up four fingers.

'Four Special International Breakfasts? Certainly, sir,' said the elderly waiter in perfect English.

They all adjusted their watches while they waited for the food.

'So,' said Jack. 'How far up the Far Northern are you going?'

'To Barents Terminus,' said Ben.

'Barents Terminus!' exclaimed Jack. 'You *have* got someone to meet you there?'

'Well . . . er . . . no,' admitted Zara.

'Are you *mad*!' cried Jack. 'Have you any idea where Barents Terminus *is*? . . . It's in the middle of the frozen sea! *The middle of nowhere!* You can't go joy-riding off to the Arctic! Dressed like you are, you'd freeze to death within five minutes of stepping outside!'

'We're *not* joy-riding!' Zara burst out. 'We have to get to Nordbergen and rescue our uncle! He's been kidnapped with his friends and we couldn't go to the police because they wouldn't believe us and our uncle will be killed if we don't rescue him before Wednesday! One of his friends left us instructions to go to Barents Terminus so that's what we're doing.'

Jack looked directly at the three children for several seconds before speaking. 'Straight up?' he asked.

'Straight up,' they said together, meeting his gaze.

Jack thought for a moment, rubbing his unshaven chin. 'Well, it might not be such a barmy plan, going to Barents Terminus,' he admitted. 'You might be able to find people to help you once you get up there. Frank and Yuri would do what they could, for a start. But I'd better come with you. I've got a daughter about your age back in England and I wouldn't like to think of her wandering about the Arctic by herself.'

'That'd be really good,' said Zara, suddenly relieved to have an adult helping them at last. 'But weren't you supposed to be going to see your family?'

''S all right,' said Jack. 'Me kids in Lahore didn't really know when I was coming, so it won't matter.'

'Didn't you say you were going to see your kids in Istanbul?' asked Ben.

'Yeah, them as well,' said Jack. 'I was gonna see them en route, like. Right,' he continued, seeming anxious to move on from the subject of his children, 'I'll need to sort meself out a new ticket.' From the side pocket of his jacket he produced what appeared to be some sort of home-made machine and placed it on the table in front of him. It was rectangular in shape, about the size of a paperback book, its grey plastic casing crudely held together with insulating tape.

From his breast pocket, Jack took a blank ticket and slid it into the machine. 'Now, then,' he muttered, tapping a row of buttons with two fingers. 'Bohemia Interchange to Barents Terminus.' The machine whirred briefly and the ticket reappeared, now with **BI———>BT** printed on it.

'Are people allowed to print out their own tickets like that?' asked Sam, somewhat surprised.

'Ah, well, I've got a special Frequent Traveller's arrangement,' said Jack, giving Sam a wink. 'Saves me queuing up at the ticket offices, like.'

'Here comes our breakfast,' said Ben, and Jack stuffed his ticket machine back into his pocket as the waiter returned with a heavily laden silver tray.

The Special International Breakfast more than lived up to Jack's recommendation. As they devoured the feast, wild high-speed music cut through the general noise of the hall. Beneath the central clock, the two musicians from their train had formed a little band with the three musicians from the Grand Orient line, the violin case set open in front of them to collect money. Their exotic musical fusion perfectly suited this subterranean international meeting place.

'I can't eat all these croissants and stuff,' said Zara, mopping up the last of her fried egg yolk with a piece of dumpling.

'I can manage one more banana fritter,' said Sam, helping himself from the pile. 'We could take the rest of this with us for the journey.'

'Good idea,' said Ben, finishing the last of his yak butter tea. 'We might . . .'

'*FIEND!*' The high-pitched cry almost made Ben drop his mug. In the centre of the hall, a bespectacled man with a bushy ginger beard was pointing his furled umbrella at a portly white-haired gentleman. They had apparently just spotted one another whilst crossing the hall from different sides, and each man's face was contorted with rage.

'*SCHWEIN!*' roared the larger man in a deeper voice, as the two men rushed at each other. The band stopped and the hall fell silent. The bearded man lunged, the white-haired man swung his briefcase wildly and the two of them ended up crashing to the floor in an undignified scuffle. Suddenly, a door flew open in the side of the clock tower and an enormous woman in a blue uniform strode out, knocked the opponents' heads together, grabbed them by their collars and dragged them back into her tower. The band started up again and the hall resumed its bustle as if nothing had happened.

'ISNT Security Police,' said Jack. 'They keep a pretty close eye on things. Those two'll be barred from travelling on the ISNT for a while.'

'But who were they?' asked Zara. 'I thought they were going to kill each other!'

'Are they secret agents?' guessed Ben. 'Working for deadly enemy powers?'

'Gawd no! You wouldn't catch secret agents brawling in public like that,' said Jack. 'No, those two were academics. Historians, probably; they're the worst.'

The waiter returned with their bill, made out in several different currencies. In sterling it came to £18. Jack fished out a handful of loose change and counted three pounds onto the saucer. 'I'm a bit short of ready cash right now,' he said. 'Could you lend me the rest of my share of the bill, just till we get to a cashpoint, like?' He had apparently forgotten his promise to buy them all breakfast but, as he was helping them, it seemed a bit rude to remind him.

'That's fine,' said Zara, taking a ten- and a five-pound note from her purse. 'Don't worry about it.' There were only three ten-pound notes left in her purse, and a few coins. After a moment's thought, she added a couple of pound coins to the saucer. Uncle Alexander always left a tip, even when they were a bit broke.

After packing the leftover croissants and fritters into their rucksacks they set off down the Far Northern passageway, at the end of which, as expected, turnstiled gateways led to and from the platform. The three children passed through ahead of Jack.

'Bloomin' machines!' The children turned round to see Jack pushing the turnstile in vain. 'Blimmin' thing won't turn,' he said, 'but it won't give me me ticket back either.'

BEEEEEP! BEEEEEP! BEEEEEP! BEEEEEP!

An alarm above the gateway burst into life. 'Strewth! That's torn it!' exclaimed Jack. 'Sorry, you'll have to go on alone. Quick! Don't let 'em think you're with me! When you get to Barents Terminus, find Frank and Yuri. They'll help you out. Good luck!' He turned and began walking quickly back towards the Central Hall.

The children lingered and saw the burly figure of the security policewoman appear round the corner. Jack was the only other person in the passageway and she made a beeline for him.

'Come on!' hissed Ben anxiously. 'Before she sees us too! He said to go without him. Look, our train's already in.'

As they approached the waiting train, they could hear Jack's voice echoing above the persistent alarm: ''Mornin' missus! Listen, I think there's something wrong with yer gate . . . I just put me ticket in and . . . hey, no, let go of me arm . . . I can go back to the ticket office and get another . . . It's no bother . . . honest!' The children looked at each other mournfully but there didn't seem to be anything they could do to help him.

This train had three carriages instead of two behind the engine. The rear carriage had no seats and was clearly for luggage. Bulky rucksacks, some bundled skis and even a small sledge lay on the floor. Most of the blue leather seats in the front two carriages were already taken by middle-aged and elderly men and women, well clad in padded jackets or fur coats. Some were pouring coffee from vacuum flasks; others were reading newspapers printed in languages, and even alphabets, which were unintelligible to the children.

They found three seats together in the front carriage and sat down without talking, reluctant to discuss Jack's arrest in the presence of strangers. They were also each half-expecting security officers to come charging down the platform and haul them off for questioning. It was a relief when, at nine o'clock precisely, the doors hissed shut and the train trundled forwards to begin its underground journey to the Far North.

Chapter Seventeen

Marcia Slick woke in an unfamiliar bed. How long had she been asleep? Felt like a long time. Then why did she feel so drowsy? Was she ill? What was that strange chemical taste in her dry mouth? Where was she? With an effort she sat up. Felt worse. Headache. Dizzy. White walls spinning. She closed her eyes and waited for the spinning to stop. Then she opened them slowly and tried to take in her surroundings. There wasn't much to take in. The bed was in one corner of a small windowless room. In the corner opposite her was a door. In the centre of the wall across from her bed was another door. Beside her was the room's only other piece of furniture, a low bedside table on which stood a clear plastic beaker of water and a white plastic vase containing six red tulips. The room was softly lit by a hemispherical light in the centre of the ceiling.

Marcia's head started spinning again as she got out of bed and stood up. She walked unsteadily over to the door in the centre of the wall. There was no handle so she pushed it but it was firmly locked. To the right of the door, a small rectangle of black plastic had been set into the wall but nothing happened when she pressed this. She noticed a tiny glazed hole high up in the door and stood on tiptoe to try and look through it. However, the hole seemed to be blocked off from the other side and she could see nothing.

She tried the other door, in the corner. This door did have a handle and opened into an even smaller room, fitted with a sink and toilet, both made of plastic. There was no mirror. She switched on the light, shut the door and used the toilet. Then she washed her hands and splashed cold water onto her face. That was better. Her brain was beginning to wake up. She went back into the bedroom and thumped on the first door with the palm of her hand. 'Hello!' she called. 'Is anybody there?' Nobody answered.

Where was she? Some kind of hospital? How had she got here? A memory of her mother floated into her brain. Her mother telling her they were taking her somewhere to make her better. And there had been a plane. They had come on a plane, last night. But *had* it been last night? What time was it now? There was no clock in the room. There was nothing to give the slightest clue to the time of day or to where on earth she might be. She wished her brain didn't feel so fuzzy inside.

The room was very warm and her mouth was terribly dry. Marcia walked back to the bedside table and brought the beaker to her lips. *STOP!* A sudden feeling that she shouldn't drink it. Why not? It looked clear. Did it smell wrong? Not exactly, but . . . But what? She seemed to *sense*, rather than smell, that this water was connected to that odd taste in her mouth. It evoked an elusive memory of something. Something unusual. Something about her mother again.

Yes, that was it – her mother had kept giving her water. Her mother *never* gave her water in the night, nor her father. Not even when she'd been little; not even when she'd been ill. She'd always been expected to sort herself out or wait for the au pair. Now other memories of last night came flooding back. Her parents had been behaving strangely all evening. They'd allowed her to go out and play football and had cooked her her favourite tea (shepherd's pie) for when she got back. Her parents' idea of cooking usually involved her father putting on a striped apron and impressing their guests by pretending to make food the caterers had prepared earlier. They never cooked for her.

And then they'd made her a mug of cocoa to take to bed. Her parents! Cocoa! She should have been more suspicious. She didn't remember reading before she fell asleep like she usually did. She didn't remember anything . . . apart from half waking up in the night. The car. Then a field. A plane. Then nothing. Not arriving, not getting off the plane, not being put in this room.

She took the beaker of water into the bathroom, poured it down the sink, rinsed it and refilled it from the cold tap. A notice above the taps said Not for Drinking but she ignored it. If someone was trying to make her drink the water they'd put by her bed, someone *would* write that, wouldn't they? Someone? Who? Her parents? She glugged down the beaker of cool tap water and filled it again. The second beaker cleared her brain of the last of its mugginess and another recent memory snapped into focus. The night before last, when her mother was being as horrible as usual, her father had said something really odd.

'Everything will be sorted out soon.'

With cold clarity, Marcia concluded that, for some reason, her parents had drugged her, driven her to an airfield, which certainly hadn't been a proper airport, and brought her here to be locked in this room and kept half asleep with more drugged water. But why? Were they planning to have cosmetic surgery done to her nose and lips against her will?

Tears spilled down her cheeks as she finally let go of a frail scrap of hope; a hope she'd been holding on to against all the odds throughout her thirteen years of life: the hope that her parents loved her. They loved the *idea* of having a daughter, a perfect daughter who didn't exist, but they didn't love *her*.

She felt anger at them and anger at herself for still wanting their love. She had to face the truth. Whatever they were doing, it wasn't normal and it wasn't right. Now she felt fear. She fought down the panic rising from her gut. She had to escape from here. She *would* escape.

She heard footsteps approaching outside. She turned off the bathroom light and hurried back to her bed. If they were trying to drug her, it would be better to make them think they were succeeding. She put the empty beaker down on the bedside table and got back into bed, sitting up but trying to look as drowsy as possible. The footsteps stopped outside the door for a few seconds. Was somebody peering through that glass hole? Then, with a soft hum the door slid sideways.

A man and a woman came into the room. The man, slim, carefully groomed and in his early forties, wore a white coat over his dark blue suit. The woman, younger and dressed in a nurse's uniform, had a rather sullen expression. She carried a blue plastic tray. The man turned and placed his thumb on the black plastic panel, causing the door to slide shut behind them.

'Good morning, Marcia,' said the man, flashing her a smarmy smile.

'Who are you? . . . Where am I?' murmured Marcia, keeping her eyes half closed.

'You're fine,' said the man. 'There's nothing to worry about, Marcia. Your mum and dad have brought you here so that we can make you better.'

'Don't feel right . . . Feel sleepy,' droned Marcia. The fact that the man seemed neither surprised nor concerned by this confirmed her suspicions.

'Just a touch of fever,' he purred. 'We'll soon have you sorted out. Why don't you have something to eat and another drink?'

As the woman placed the tray on the table, her digital watch was just visible to Marcia. The time was 11.30 a.m.

On the tray was a bowl of soup with a bread roll and a plastic beaker of coke. Marcia sat up in bed and put the tray on her knee. 'Mmm, I am hungry,' she said, trying to sound drowsy and enthusiastic at the same time, and scooped a spoonful of soup to her mouth. 'Bit hot,' she said, barely touching the soup with her lips. It wasn't too hot but it was likely to be drugged, she decided. She took a bite from the roll instead. Dry food was less likely to be tampered with. What if they stayed to watch her eat the whole meal? To her relief they turned and went back to the door.

'You get as much sleep as you feel like,' said the man, as the woman used her thumb to activate the door. 'It'll make you feel better.'

Marcia caught only a glimpse of another white wall and a blue lino-covered floor before the door slid shut behind them. Footsteps receded down what Marcia guessed to be some sort of corridor. Only one set of footsteps though, Marcia thought. She took a spoonful of soup into her mouth but didn't swallow it. Another set of footsteps padded quietly away and, fairly sure she was no longer being watched, she spat the mouthful back into the bowl. Then she got out of bed, poured the soup and the coke down the toilet, and replaced the empty bowl and beaker on the tray. She scraped the spoon around the bowl a few times to give the impression that the soup had been eaten rather than tipped, and ate the rest of the roll. Then she began to examine the two rooms again, desperately looking for some way out.

In many books Marcia had read, people were imprisoned in rooms conveniently provided with ventilation shafts or chimneys one could clamber through. However, a thorough search of the bedroom and toilet failed to reveal

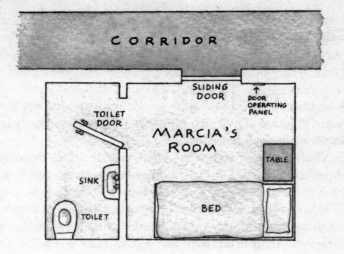

any such means of escape. There wasn't even anything which could be turned into a sharp tool or weapon, she realized. The soup spoon, the beakers, the bowl and the flower vase were all made of plastic. The room contained none of her possessions from home. She had no clothes other than the pyjamas she wore.

After a fruitless half-hour of searching, she heard footsteps approaching again. She jumped into bed and lay under the duvet, pretending to be sound asleep. The footsteps stopped for a moment before the door slid open and the woman entered. Through almost-closed eyes, Marcia watched her place a new beaker of water on the table, pick up the tray and leave.

As the door slid shut, something occurred to Marcia. For those few seconds in which the woman had been in the room collecting the tray, she had left the door open behind her. A plan began to form in Marcia's mind.

Chapter Eighteen

'Is it lunchtime?' asked Ben, as the train moved on from Baltic Junction. Their five remaining fellow passengers had begun to unpack large picnics.

'Wish we had a copy of Jack's map,' said Zara, as she unpacked the food. 'I can't remember exactly which way the Far Northern goes to get to Barents Terminus.'

'It goes up under Poland, Lithuania, Latvia and Estonia,' said Ben. 'Then under Finland and I think a bit of Russia. I tried to memorize that bit of the map when he was showing us. I think the stop before Barents Terminus is called Rybachiy Pol-something, so we should know when we're nearly there.'

'Wow!' said Sam, impressed. '*I* couldn't have remembered all that. And the map didn't even have the names of the countries on it.'

'Ben's a walking atlas,' said Zara proudly.

'I wish we'd bought a drink,' said Sam, after a while. 'I'm really thirsty.'

'Yeah, me too,' said Ben. 'And I reckon it's going to be hours before we get to Barents Terminus. We've got to go further than we travelled yesterday.'

'Haluaisitko kupin teeta?' An elderly woman sitting a few seats away from Zara was smiling and passing them an enormous vacuum flask and a plastic cup. In spite of the language barrier, her meaning was clear.

'Thank you,' said Zara, reaching across to take the flask and cup. 'Would you like some of these banana fritters?'

'Kiitos!' said the woman, beaming, and took one.

They were doing all right, Zara told herself, as they shared the warm sweet tea. They could do nothing to help Uncle Alexander until they reached Barents Terminus and found Frank and Yuri. Whoever they might be.

Chapter Nineteen

Marcia Slick sawed several more strands of hair from the back of her head. She carefully laid them onto the long bunch she had already accumulated on the bedside table. A few loose hairs drifted down onto the cream carpet. She picked them up meticulously. She had cut the hair from the back, hoping that her long hair would look normal from the front to whoever came in with the next meal. *If* anyone came in with the next meal. It was impossible to know what time it was but she guessed it was now late afternoon and she was assuming they'd bring her more food at some point.

The hardest part of her plan had been finding something sharp enough to cut her hair. After searching in vain for metal brackets along the underside of the bed, she had finally thought of somewhere she might find some glass. With much difficulty she had prised off the plastic casing of the tiny strip light above the toilet sink. She had extracted the short tubular light bulb and smashed it on the inside rim of the toilet, leaving her with a shard of glass protruding from one metal end. As an implement for cutting hair, it was unsafe and unwieldy but, somehow, she had managed the job without injuring her fingers, neck or scalp.

Footsteps approached outside. Trying not to panic, trying not to lose any more hairs, Marcia twisted the length of hair together and hid it under the mattress. She hid her makeshift knife behind the leg of the bed. Then she got into bed and shut her eyes. The footsteps stopped. After a few seconds' pause, the door slid open and the woman entered the room. Balancing the tray on her left hand and arm, she closed the door behind her. Marcia had expected that. If they were bringing her a meal, she was presumably due to be waking up from the previous dose of sleeping drug.

Marcia opened her eyes, yawned and sat up slowly. 'Thanks,' she mumbled. Sleepy and compliant; that was the impression she needed to convey. The woman placed the tray down without speaking. Shepherd's pie and peas, and a glass of orange juice.

As the woman left the room, Marcia took a mouthful of juice, spitting it out once she heard the woman walk away. Marcia looked at the meal. All of it might be drugged but she was absolutely starving. She ate the peas and looked longingly at the shepherd's pie. If *she* were drugging a shepherd's pie she'd put it in the mince, she decided. She carefully ate some of the mashed potato; only half of it, in case she was wrong.

After flushing everything else down the toilet, she got to work on the bed. First she removed the duvet cover. Then she rolled up the duvet and arranged it on the bed to look something like the shape of a person sleeping on their side, facing the wall. Next, she splayed the hair across the pillow. Finally, she covered the crude dummy with the cover, leaving only a bit of the hair-covered pillow showing, as if the sleeper had their head right down under the duvet.

She stood back, by the door. Would it fool the woman? The duvet cover was a bit too thin, she thought, but it might go unnoticed. Generally the effect was pretty good.

She considered her broken light bulb. After some thought, she hid it under the bed. She didn't want to take it with her. Apart from the fact that she hated violence, the jagged glass would be more of a danger to herself than to anyone else.

Finally, she took the plastic fork out of the bowl and put it on the table, beside the tray. Picking it up would probably only delay the woman by another half-second but it might be the extra half-second Marcia needed. An extra half-second during which the woman would have her back to the sliding door. And the toilet.

Marcia went into the dark toilet and hid behind the half-open door. Through the crack between the hinges she could just see the sliding door. With nothing else to do but wait, Marcia began to worry. What if the woman saw her with her peripheral vision? Maybe she should crawl. No. Too slow. When she got out she should turn left; the foot-steps always came and went from the right. Then she should hide, quickly. But what if the corridor was full of people? What if there was nowhere to hide? What if the woman turned and saw her before she was through the door? What if (and this was the biggest if) the woman didn't leave the door open all this time? Stop panicking, she told herself. How long had it been now? Fifteen minutes? Half an hour?

At last. Footsteps. The usual pause outside. Door sliding open. Woman walking in. *Leave it open. Leave it open . . .* No. The woman turned and pressed the thumb panel, shutting the door before moving out of Marcia's narrow field of vision. Damn! Would the dummy fool her anyway? What was she doing? Had she seen something was wrong? Was she reaching for the duvet cover? No, here she was, leaving the room with the tray.

The door slid shut. As the woman's footsteps faded away, Marcia let out a long, shaky breath. She was trembling, her heart was pounding and her legs felt weak. She emerged from the bathroom and, in a rush of frustration, threw herself at the sliding door. Biting her lip, she pummelled at the smooth metal with her fists. She wanted to scream, wanted to throw that stupid vase of tulips across the room, smash that table against the wall, take the broken glass knife and . . . and . . .

No! She mustn't go berserk. She *mustn't*. She had to keep a grip on herself; had to continue to fool them that she was being drugged successfully. It was her only chance of escaping from this hateful room. She sat on the bed, wiping tears from her face with her pyjama sleeve. She *would* get another chance. The woman would leave the door open next time. Or the time after. The dummy had worked. Would there have been enough time to get out if the door had been open? Yes, Marcia decided. Just.

But what if there were to be no more meals brought in? Surely they weren't planning to keep her here for ever? Why had they kept her in here for so long already? No way of guessing when she didn't even know where she was. Or why they had brought her here. Or what they were going to . . . *No*. Don't think about that. Pointless. Stay calm. Stay prepared. If or when the woman came back with breakfast, Marcia would be ready. With painstaking care, Marcia began to gather up the strands of hair from the pillow.

Chapter Twenty

It was 8.30 p.m. when the train finally rattled into Barents Terminus. The children were the only people in their carriage, the last of their fellow passengers having disembarked at Rybachiy Poluostrov, an hour and a half earlier.

'Well, here we are,' said Zara, putting on her rucksack as the train doors hissed open. The boys followed her onto the platform. There was nobody waiting to get on and they could now see that the other two carriages were also empty of people and luggage.

As they walked towards the platform's exit gate, the train doors hissed shut. The train trundled round its circular overhead rail and disappeared back into the tunnel. The children turned to watch the red rear light vanish. The clickety-click became faster and faster yet quieter and quieter, until the sound faded away to nothing. Silence. No sound of human activity. Not a soul to be seen.

The walls of the round chamber were functionally decorated in plain white tiling and the

◆ BARENTS TERMINUS ◆

signs were white with black lettering. The children made their way through the plain black turnstile gate. Automatically Zara turned to collect her ticket from the slot but their tickets were retained by the machine. This was the end of the line; the end of their journey on the ISNT.

The short passage led them to a large grey metal lift.

'It's a big lift for a station that doesn't seem to be used much,' observed Zara as they began to ascend.

'Probably so people can fit their skis and sledges and stuff in,' guessed Ben, remembering the luggage compartment on their train, and Zara was reminded how ill-equipped they were for this part of the world. They didn't even have any food left. Lunch seemed a very long time ago now.

After a long ascent, the lift stopped. The door opened onto an empty room. The plywood wall opposite was featureless, except for a small brass button in its centre.

'Well, here goes,' said Sam, pressing it. Two things hit their senses as the wall slid sideways: the smell of rope, and the cold. The air wasn't freezing but, after the warm underground atmosphere of the ISNT, it was definitely chilly.

'We're in some sort of big storeroom,' said Ben, as they walked through into a dimly lit space between two rows of tall shelving. 'Look at all this stuff.'

The shelves were piled high with skis, oil drums, coils of ropes, wooden crates, torches, boots and gloves. The plywood wall slid shut behind them. As at Bright & Buffwelle, the way through to the lift was concealed, in this case by a rail of ancient-looking fur snowsuits. The children walked along between the shelves, out into a more open area of the room.

A large motorized sled stood on the concrete floor. Its slightly battered red metal body was boat-shaped, about four metres long and a metre and a half wide, and lay low to the ground. There was an enclosed cab at the front, with an open section behind it. Right at the back was the engine, with a rubber-tracked drive belt hanging down underneath.

'Wow!' said Sam, going over for a closer look. 'I reckon this works as a boat as well as a snowmobile. See, there's a propeller raised up at the back here under the engine and –'

'Don't touch it!' said Zara. 'You don't know what it might do. D'you think we're in some sort of cellar?' She looked around for some steps.

'No,' said Ben. The vehicle was facing a wide metal door and Ben had walked across to peer through the door's small window. 'We're at ground level; or rather, sea level.' Sam and Zara joined him.

After nineteen hours underground, it was refreshing to see the sky again; a beautiful, clear night sky, bejewelled with thousands of stars. The scene beneath the sky was beautiful too: a rugged plain of snow-covered ice stretching away into the darkness. Beautiful, but frightening at the same time. For several seconds, no one said anything.

Ben rattled the door. 'Locked,' he said.

'We couldn't go out dressed like this anyway,' Zara pointed out. 'We'd freeze to death in five minutes, Jack said.'

Sam noticed something. 'There's some sort of flickering light out there,' he said. 'I can't see it properly; it's coming from somewhere round the other side of the building.'

They all peered sideways through the window. Sam was right. It was barely perceivable from this viewpoint but they could just make out a shimmering, dancing white glare, spilling here and there onto raised bumps in the ice.

'It could be the Aurora Borealis!' exclaimed Zara. 'You know – the Northern Lights.'

'Pity there aren't any windows on the other side of this building,' said Ben, looking round.

The desolate scene outside, with its unexplained illuminations, only increased the eerie mood of this strange, silent place. Were they supposed to be here? Then why was there no one here? What was this place? The room was basically a single circular space, except for the screened-off lift area. The room's rounded wall had been built from great sheets of metal, fastened together with massive rivets and coated in thick white paint. The sturdy industrial effect reminded Sam of the inside of a car ferry but the shape reminded him of something else.

'Look,' he said. 'The walls are tapering towards the ceiling. It's like we're inside a lighthouse.'

'There must be an upstairs,' said Zara. '*Somebody* must be here.'

'There!' said Ben, pointing into the shadows behind the shelves. Fixed to the wall, leading up to a round trapdoor in the high ceiling, was a metal ladder.

'Come on,' said Zara and, with Ben and Sam following, she began to climb.

'Hello,' she called, knocking on the trapdoor. 'Is anyone there?' But nobody answered. Zara pushed the door upwards. A warm light. A delicious meaty smell. A faint bubbling sound. She pushed the trapdoor open on its hinge and clambered up, emerging through the floor of another round room, which was clearly a kitchen.

'Bit warmer up here,' said Ben as he and Sam joined his sister. The heat, as well as the smell and sounds of cooking, was emanating from a black stove, connected to a bulky blue Calor gas cylinder. In the wood-lined wall of the kitchen, above the fitted cupboards and sink, was a single porthole window.

'Hello!' called Zara again. It felt wrong to just barge in like this. But still, nobody answered. Homely though this kitchen was, the odd absence of people was making her nervy.

'Let's have a look at these Northern Lights,' said Ben. 'I reckon this porthole faces the opposite direction to those doors downstairs.'

They looked out but there were no Northern Lights. The spectacle they beheld did not resemble any Arctic phenomenon they'd ever read about. Below them, a huge square of silvery light lay spread across the side of a snow-drift. Within the square moved the images of two men. One man was big and fat with a small moustache. The other was thin and wore a rather vacant expression. They were trying to manhandle a piano up a long flight of stone steps. From somewhere above them, someone was projecting a Laurel and Hardy film onto the snow.

'This is really weird,' said Zara.

'But it proves there's *definitely* someone here,' said Ben. He pointed to another ladder on the wall behind them. 'Let's go on up.'

The trapdoor opened onto a small landing with three closed doors leading off it but it was from the floor above them that they could now hear human sounds – the sound of Oliver Hardy berating Stan Laurel accompanied by the noise of hysterical laughter.

Another ladder and another trapdoor brought the children into a circular living room. There were no lights on and the room's big windows offered a fabulous 360° view of the surrounding icy wilderness. On the far side of the room two men were sitting at either side of a whirring film projector. They sat right up close to one of the windows, leaning forwards in their seats and looking out, shaking, howling and cackling with laughter. Sam had watched this film once on television with his dad and guessed that the piano had just gone rolling back down the steps for the umpteenth time.

The children looked at each other nervously. 'Er . . . excuse me . . .' said Zara tentatively.

The two men jumped to their feet and turned round. 'Goodness me!' said the man on the left. 'We have visitors.' He switched off the projector and the other man switched on a table lamp beside him. Both men were very old, well into their eighties. The man who had spoken had wispy white hair and wore gold-rimmed spectacles. The other man had neither hair nor glasses but spectacularly spidery white eyebrows, now raised high in his creviced forehead as he beamed at the children. Both men wore crumpled blue boiler suits over polo-necked jerseys.

'I'm sorry,' said the man with the spectacles. He took them off and wiped his eyes with a pocket handkerchief. 'We mustn't have heard the lift-arrival buzzer.' He replaced his glasses and walked towards the children, hand extended. 'I'm Frank and this is Yuri,' he said. 'Welcome to Barents Terminus.'

Chapter Twenty-One

'*You've got to help us! Our uncle's been kidnapped!*'

'*They're going to kill him!*'

'Jack told us to find you! Professor Gauntraker –'

'Eric Gauntraker?' exclaimed Frank. 'Is he here with you?

'No, he was kidnapped too, with the others! He sort of told us to come here when . . .'

'*We have to rescue them!*'

'We've only got until Wednesday! They're going to be . . .'

'Don't all speak at once!' cried Frank. 'Now, who's been kidnapped? By whom? When did this happen? Where did –'

'Wait, Frank!' interrupted Yuri, holding Frank's arm with a brawny brown hand. 'Look at them. They are exhausted.' He spoke in a thick Russian accent as his dark eyes scrutinized the children's faces. 'Hungry, too. You have travelled a long way, yes?'

'Yes,' said Zara. 'From Edinburgh. But our uncle –'

'Come. You can tell it all whilst we eat,' declared Yuri, as his head disappeared down the trapdoor. 'Always things look better after food. Everything will turn out nice again. You see.'

'Yuri's learnt most of his English from our old film library,' smiled Frank, shepherding the children down the ladder. 'George Formby's a big favourite.'

They sat around a wooden table in the warm kitchen. Yuri ladled out five bowls of stew and dumplings. 'Reindeer casserole,' he announced proudly. 'Real Arctic cuisine.'

As the hot food began to fill their stomachs, Zara told Frank and Yuri everything that had happened: the sudden arrival of Professor Gauntraker, the story of the University of Nordbergen, the summoning of the other four professors, Professor Gauntraker's interrupted explanation, the violent kidnapping, the secret instructions in the button and their journey to Barents Terminus on the ISNT. Ben and Sam chipped in occasionally when they thought she was missing something out and, by the time everyone had finished their stew, Frank and Yuri had been given a pretty full account.

'So Eric was right,' said Yuri, looking grim.

'Eric Gauntraker passed through here a couple of months ago,' explained Frank. 'Told us he was going to Nordbergen to investigate rumours. Rumours which led him to suspect that Professor Murdo had returned there.'

'Eric is old pal of ours,' said Yuri. 'We have been seeing him often, over the years, making his Arctic expeditions.'

'Right,' announced Frank, standing up and clapping his hands together. 'Action stations. Operation Rescue Mission. You load up the ski-boat, Yuri, and I'll draw up an assault plan. First thing tomorrow, we'll –'

'Hold the horses, Frank,' interrupted Yuri. 'We cannot just rush off to Nordbergen. Is beyond a day's range for ski-boat. And we are too few against Murdo's men. We would all be killed.'

Zara's spirits sank. Had they come all this way for nothing?

'We need reinforcements,' continued Yuri, standing up. 'I will radio Olaf.'

'Of course,' said Frank. 'Good thinking.'

'Who's Olaf?' asked Zara.

'Norwegian police officer,' said Frank. 'Based on Petrøya. Wait,' he said, noticing the children's blank faces. 'I'll show you.' He took a map from a flat drawer in the kitchen table and laid it out.

Svalbard

Prins
Karls
Forlandet

Spisbergen

Nordaustlandet

Longyearbyen

Kong Karls
Landet

Barentsøya

Edgeøya

Hopen

Bjørnøya

Petrøya

Kvitøya

Zemlya Frantsa Iosifa

Ostrov
Greem-Bell

Zemlya Vilcheka

Zemlya
Aleksandry

Zemlya
Georgu

Nordbergen

Novoya Zemlya

Barents Sea

MINIMUM SUMMER EXTENT OF SEA ICE

MAXIMUM WINTER EXTENT OF SEA ICE

Barents
Terminus

Hammerfest

NORWAY

Vardø

Kolguyev

Murmansk

FINLAND

Kola
Peninsular

Sea

ARCTIC CIRCLE

White

RUSSIA

Arkhangelsk

0   100   200 300   400 km

0   100   200 miles

ARCTIC CIRCLE

'See?' said Frank, pointing. 'We're here and Nordbergen is here, about 450 miles north-north-east of us. And this is Petrøya: 250 miles north-west of here and about 350 miles to the south-west of Nordbergen. Small island on the western fringe of the Svalbard group; governed by Norway. Petrøya's sole police officer, Olaf Nansen, is a pal of Yuri's.'

'I go there sometimes in summer,' said Yuri. 'Play chess. I radio him now.'

'But one police officer won't be able to do much more than we would against all of Professor Murdo's men!' said Zara, anxiously, as Yuri started climbing the ladder.

'Ah, but Nansen will be able to contact the authorities in Norway for help,' said Frank.

'He's a good man,' declared Yuri, disappearing up through the trapdoor hole. 'I will convince him situation is urgent. I make him call out Norwegian Special Forces, jet planes, parachute soldiers – whatever we need.'

'Murdo's men won't be any sort of match for the rescue force Yuri will make Olaf summon,' said Frank when Yuri had gone.

The children smiled at each other encouragingly, keeping their doubts to themselves. Could these two old men really conjure up such powerful assistance? Would it really be possible for these Norwegian forces to rescue the prisoners alive?

'Do you have a phone here as well as the radio?' asked Sam, hoping he'd be able to try ringing his parents again.

'No, we've never really had the need for a telephone,' said Frank. 'In the days when telephones needed cables, radio was the more practical option up here in the Arctic. Yuri says we should look into these new satellite phones but I'm afraid I'm too old-fashioned to get round to it.'

'Have you and Yuri been living here for a long time?' asked Zara, as Frank poured them each a mug of tea.

'Decades,' answered Frank. 'Yuri and I must be two of the longest-serving employees on the entire ISNT network, and that's saying something.'

'So you were here thirty-five years ago when our uncle and Professor Gauntraker and the others had been stranded on the ice by Professor Murdo?' asked Ben. 'They did come here then, didn't they?'

'Oh yes. Remember the occasion well,' said Frank. 'They were very lucky that Professor Murdo left them less than ten miles from here. Chance in a thousand. And if we'd happened to have had the lights on, Murdo would have spotted us and flown on to dump them somewhere else. They were nearly done in anyway. Ten miles is a long way to walk across the ice in the dark.'

'Do polar explorers often use this ISNT station?' asked Sam.

'We get a fair few passing through,' said Frank. 'Mind you, the builders of the Far Northern Line never intended this to be a remote terminus. They were hoping to find a natural tunnel right under the Arctic Ocean to Canada or Greenland, but the tiny rock on which this tower stands was as far as they could get.'

'It must be a bit strange living here in the middle of the ice all the time,' Zara remarked.

'Oh, we occasionally make trips in the ski-boat to other islands in the Barents Sea,' said Frank. 'Such as Yuri's chess expeditions to Petrøya.'

'But doesn't the ISNT station have to be kept secret?' asked Ben.

'Absolutely,' grinned Frank. 'To Arctic people, we're known as a couple of eccentrics living in an old weather station, conducting a lifelong survey of the sea birds. Ah, here's Yuri.'

Yuri slid down the ladder, one foot on each side, with graceful ease. 'I cannot make contact with Petrøya,' he said, frowning. 'No reception from Olaf's office radio at all.'

'Isn't there another radio on Petrøya?' asked Sam.

'Yes, there is radio room at a big inn called Bjørn's Bar. I try this too, but also is totally dead.'

'That's odd,' said Frank. 'They generally keep their set switched on round the clock. Well, no doubt we'll get through if we try a bit later.' His confident tone now seemed just a tiny bit forced, Zara thought, and anxiety crept back into her stomach like a cold fog.

'But what if we *don't* get through?' she pressed. 'What if we can't contact him in time at all?'

'We will,' said Yuri. 'Always Olaf is based on Petrøya. Is his duty. Probably he is making repair to Petrøya radio mast right now. Probably that is it. Don't worry. We will try all night.'

'How about contacting the Norwegian authorities directly?' suggested Sam.

'Trouble is, they don't *know* us,' Frank pointed out. 'We'd have as much difficulty persuading them to take the necessary action as you would have done persuading the Edinburgh police. They might *half*-believe us and send a helicopter to have a look at Nordbergen, but that could merely endanger the lives of your uncle and the others still further. No, we need to speak to Olaf. I'm sure we'll get through to him soon.'

'But we can't just *wait*!' exploded Zara. This was awful. They were back to square one.

'Couldn't we go to Petrøya in the ski-boat and speak to Olaf in person?' said Ben. 'It's not as far as Nordbergen, is it?'

Frank and Yuri looked at each other, considering. Please say yes, thought Zara. Anything would be better than waiting around doing nothing.

'Is possible,' said Yuri, at last.

'All right,' said Frank. 'If we haven't got through to Olaf by first thing tomorrow morning – though I'm pretty sure we will have – Yuri can drive the three of you over to Petrøya. I'll stay here to man the ISNT station and keep trying to radio Olaf anyway. I can keep in touch with you on the ski-boat radio. It's safe enough at this time of year: the sea ice is still reasonably firm and we get twelve hours of daylight just now, though the sun never gets very high. If you set off at first light you should make it comfortably before darkness falls.'

'At least we'd be sure of speaking to Olaf,' said Zara. 'But he won't have much time to organize the rescue.'

'Don't worry,' said Frank. 'He's very efficient. Now then, you'd better all go up to your sleeping quarters and get a good night's kip. We always keep a few beds made up in the attic for any polar explorers who blow in.'

'Sleep good,' said Yuri as the children made their way up the ladder. 'Probably certainly I get through to Olaf in night. Everything will be hunky and dory. You see. But if we have to go to Petrøya, we leave at the cracking of dawn. So you sleep.'

Less than an hour later, the three of them were lying in their beds in the cosy round room at the top of the tower. Ben lay awake, looking up at the shadowy coned ceiling above them. Sam and Zara were already asleep but he felt restless. Had Uncle Alexander and the others slept in this room, thirty-five years ago, exhausted from their gruelling trek? Probably. Ben desperately wished his uncle could be here now, safe and well and with them. Maybe Yuri and

Frank were right: maybe, by the end of tomorrow, his uncle and the others would be free. But he couldn't rid his mind of the thought that, if all their plans failed, tomorrow would be Uncle Alexander's last day alive.

Ben got out of bed and padded across to one of the double-glazed portholes. He looked out over the starlit frozen seascape. Somewhere out there beyond the horizon, 450 miles across the ice, his kind, lovely Uncle Alexander was being held prisoner by those horrible, evil men.

Well, he resolved, even if they couldn't find Olaf, even if they couldn't find anyone to help them, even if they had to walk over every mile of ice from Petrøya to Nordbergen, they were going to rescue his uncle and they would never give up.

Chapter Twenty-Two

Tap tap tap! A flock of ravens. Sharp beaks hammering on the French window. Glass starting to crack. Run! Way blocked. Turnstile won't turn. Ticket won't go in! Wrong ticket! Tap tap tap!

Sam woke suddenly and opened his eyes. For a few seconds he struggled to free his mind from the horrible dream and remember where he was. Though it was dark, it was not quite pitch black, and he sat up to take in his surroundings. Of course. Barents Terminus. The attic room.

The tapping was coming from the underside of the trapdoor, accompanied by Yuri's voice: 'Good morning! It is time to be rising and shining. Breakfast in five minutes.'

Sam looked out of the portholes at the dark blue sky. What time was it?

Zara switched on her bedside lamp and swung her legs out of bed. 'Four-thirty,' she said, glancing at her watch. 'Looks like we're going to Petrøya.'

'Yep,' agreed Ben, already half dressed. 'Let's get a move on.'

'Still no contact with Petrøya,' confirmed Yuri, down in the kitchen. 'But don't worry. We will find Olaf when we get there.' He slopped hot porridge into their bowls. 'Eat plenty,' he advised. 'Then go down to storeroom to be properly kit up. Your clothes – no good for Arctic.'

'Morning,' called Frank, looking up at the children as they descended the ladder. He was loading a crate of tinned food into the open section of the ski-boat, which was already packed with supplies and equipment: a tin box labelled EMERGENCY FLARES, a large toolbox, petrol cans, a pair of skis and ski-poles, several coils of rope, a shovel, two ice axes and various other wooden boxes and canvas bags. 'You shouldn't need most of this stuff but it's as well to be fully prepared in this part of the world,' he said as  they joined him by the ski-boat. 'Now, give me a hand with this cover and then we'll get your togs sorted out.'

They helped Frank fasten a green tarpaulin cover over the supplies before following him over to the shelves. 'We've built up a fairly good stash of outdoor clothing here,' said Frank. 'Handy for helping out any ISNT travellers who arrive a bit unprepared. Old stuff mostly, donated by explorers on their way home. Not much small enough for youngsters but I expect we can make do. First, put on as many extra layers of your own clothes as you have in those rucksacks.' As they did this, Frank bustled about the shelves, rummaging for an item of clothing here, picking out a pair of gloves there, and ten minutes later the three children had been fully equipped. They each wore two new layers over their own clothes: soft, fleece-lined overalls under a one-piece padded snowsuit. All the legs and arms had to be rolled up a bit but they just about fitted. As well as the snowsuit hoods, they wore woollen balaclavas, and their hands were also doubly clad, in woollen fingerless gloves and chunky waterproof mittens. Three pairs of plastic snow boots had been made to more or less fit by wearing several pairs of thick woollen socks.

'You won't need all this on once the cab warms up,' said Frank, 'but you'll be glad of every last layer if you have to get out to spend a penny. Minus forty degrees centigrade it is, just now. Oh – here – you'd better take these to protect your eyes from snow glare.' He handed them three pairs of tinted goggles. They tried them on and waddled around in their full gear, looking like rather tubby aliens.

Yuri appeared at the top of the ladder, also clad in snow-suit, boots and gloves. He carried a long oilskin case on his back. 'It will be light enough soon,' he called, sliding down the full four metres of ladder. 'Let's go!'

He strode across to the ski-boat and strapped the oilskin case to an upright bracket on the outside of the cab, behind the driver's door. 'Gun,' he said. 'In case of polar bears.'

'You shoot polar bears?' exclaimed Zara, rather shocked.

'Don't worry,' said Frank. 'We've never shot anything in all the years we've been living here. It's illegal to shoot a polar bear except as an absolute last resort. But everyone must carry a gun in these parts, just in case.'

'Polar bear, big meat eater,' said Yuri. 'Not bad; just hungry. To him, you just like seal.'

'Especially dressed like this,' said Ben.

'Take care,' said Frank as he and Yuri hugged each other. Frank shook each of the children's mittened hands firmly. 'You mustn't worry,' he said. 'You three have done remarkably well, you know; getting here from Edinburgh all by yourselves. A fine show. Your uncle will be very proud of you when he's rescued.'

He quickly donned an old snowsuit and gloves himself, before rolling open the metal door. Even standing several metres from the doorway, the children were instantly struck by the unbelievably cold air. It seemed to suck every bit of heat from their exposed faces, from the bones beneath the skin, from their very insides. So this was what minus forty felt like.

Wasting no time, Frank and Yuri pushed the ski-boat across to the doorway, to the edge of a snow-covered ramp leading down to the ice. A dim twilight washed the starry sky. Eggshell blue and the faintest pink encroached from the eastern horizon.

'You three in first,' instructed Yuri and the children clambered into the enclosed cab with their rucksacks. 'Two in back, navigator in front next to me. Seat belts on.'

'Go on Ben,' said Zara, sitting next to Sam on the long seat behind the driver. 'You have first go in the front. You're best at map reading.'

Frank and Yuri shoved the ski-boat onto the ramp and, as it slid forward, Yuri swung himself into the cab, slammed the door and turned the ignition key. The engine coughed, spluttered and clattered into life. As they glided out onto the ice, Yuri wrenched down a lever to engage the drive belt.

The children looked back through the rear window. Through the tail-plume of snow spray they had their first proper view of the strange metal tower, its outside painted a dull red, standing on its lonely rock in the frozen sea.

They saw Frank braving the cold to give them a final wave from the doorway.

The ski-boat sped over the ice, its single headlamp casting a long beam ahead of them. It was exhilarating to zoom over the undulating surface, the vehicle bouncing continuously on its well-sprung ski-supports.

'Here, it is good to drive on,' said Yuri, steering expertly round the larger outcrops of ice. 'We make good speed while we can. Later, ice may be more difficult.'

Keeping one hand on the steering wheel and his eyes fixed ahead, Yuri reached beneath the dashboard and handed a grey rectangular object to Ben. It had a small screen on the front, set between several buttons.

'Wow! Is that a GPS?' Sam asked.

'It is,' confirmed Yuri. 'All mod-cons here. Global Positioning Satellite device is more accurate than old magnetic compass. See if you three can work out by self. Plugs into ceiling; aerial on roof.'

Sam and Zara leaned forward as Ben plugged the aerial cable into a socket above him. Sam had read about GPS devices and was dying to see one in action. 'Switch it on there,' he suggested and the screen flickered into life, revealing a map of the Barents Sea, similar to the one Frank had shown them. A set of latitude and longitude co-ordinates appeared across the top of the screen: 72° 12' 18" N, 38° 28' 15" E. Next to the tiny unmarked rock of Barents Terminus, a white dot pulsated.

'That's us,' said Sam. 'If we can zoom in to a larger scale, I reckon we'll see the dot moving.'

Sure enough, once Ben had pressed the button marked with a + and closed in on their section of sea, the pulsating dot moved slowly on a north-north-westerly course, trailing a growing line behind it, to mark the route they had travelled.

'It is the knees of the bee,' said Yuri proudly.

'It's amazing,' agreed Ben. 'Though do you think we should copy our course onto a real map as we go, just in case? So we know where we are if it stops working.'

Yuri shrugged. 'GPS guaranteed always working. But is good you practise mapping skills if you like. Map behind my seat, in pocket.'

Zara found the old folded map and took a pencil from her rucksack. 'I'll copy our position down every few minutes,' she said.

By now, the sun had just become visible: the top of a glowing red disc crept along the horizon on their right-hand side, rising slowly into a clear pink sky. The low sunlight splashed across the icescape like rosé wine and cast long purpley-blue shadows behind every tiny bump, every snowdrift, every wind-carved peak.

'Look!' exclaimed Sam, suddenly spotting a white dog-like animal moving across the distant ice ahead of them. 'What is it? Looks too small for a wolf.'

'It's an arctic fox!' said Zara.

Quickly, Sam dug his binoculars out of his rucksack and they each had a closer look at the short-legged fox trotting confidently on its way, until the ski-boat had left it far behind.

Scooshing through this fabulously illuminated wonderland, it was impossible for the children not to feel more optimistic than they had the night before.

Chapter Twenty-Three

Marcia Slick awoke from a dream-troubled but undrugged night's sleep to find her breakfast already there beside the bed. Damn! How long had it been there? What if the woman came back for the tray before she was ready? Quick – muesli, toast, orange juice: down the toilet. Plate, bowl, glass back on the tray. Duvet cover off. Roll duvet up. Not like that – bend its knees . . . there . . . better. Get hair from under mattress. On pillow. Don't drop any loose strands. That's it. Now the duvet cover. There. As good as yesterday? Good enough.

Into the toilet. No, take something off the tray first. The toast plate. Now into the toilet. Behind the door. Need a pee. What if the woman comes? Too bad – have a pee, quick. Need to think clearly. There. Don't flush it – she'd hear the cistern refilling. *Footsteps*. Quick, back behind the door.

The pause. Door sliding open. Woman in . . . and walking to the bedside table. *She's left the door open! Go, go, go!*

With barely a glance at the woman, Marcia sped silently out of the toilet in a sort of crouching run and through the open doorway. She turned sharply left. The corridor was straight and very long, with other doorways along the same side as her own.

Hide, quick. Get to nearest doorway. Door locked. Get flat against it. Woman coming. Get further back. Stomach in. Feet must be sticking out. Woman in corridor. Whirr of door sliding shut. *Don't look this way. Don't look this way.* Footsteps moving away. Fading away. A distant door whirring open and shut. Silence.

Marcia allowed herself to breathe out. She was trembling. Cautiously, very slowly, she peeked into the corridor and looked in both directions. There was no one about.

Her room was approximately halfway along the windowless corridor. The end to her left was closed off by another door. The other end, where the woman had gone, appeared to lead eventually into a more open space. It was hard to tell from this distance, but Marcia had the impression that this space was daylit. Her urge to find a window, to see where she was, to get out, overrode her fear of running into the woman. Keeping close to the right-hand wall, hoping she could press herself into another doorway if she heard anyone coming, she began to walk along the corridor.

She felt very conspicuous and vulnerable in her yellow pyjamas. She shivered although, like her room, the corridor was uncomfortably warm. Every door she passed was closed and handleless, with a black plastic thumb panel beside each one. Were there other people being kept prisoner here?

As Marcia neared the end of the corridor she could see that it would bring her into a wide room. Across an empty expanse of blue carpet was another corridor, directly opposite her own. To her left, spanning the distance between the two corridors, was a pale wood-veneered wall, with three doors set into it. From her restricted viewpoint in the narrow corridor, Marcia couldn't see the side of the room opposite the veneered wall at all. However, she could tell from the gridded rectangles of sunlight being cast onto the pale wood that the other wall must have a large window in it.

Was there anyone in the room? No sounds. No human shadows.

Marcia peered round the end of the corridor.

She gasped. The view which met her eyes through the metal framework of an enormous curved window left her stunned. She was high up, very high, looking out over a desolate snow-covered wilderness that stretched away to the distant horizon.

Where on earth was she? For a second she thought of the Alps, where her parents had taken her skiing. But this was no mountain range. Too flat. Way too flat. And there was something else strange. Something about the sun. Surely it was midmorning, yet the orange sun hung low in the sky. Had she misread the woman's watch? Or had her body clock got completely out of synch since yesterday?

Was she in a very tall building or was the building standing on high ground? The window took up almost the entire wall and came low to the floor. If she went right up to it and looked down, she'd get a better view of her immediate surroundings and maybe a better idea of how to find the building's exit. Feeling very exposed, Marcia left the corridor and padded towards the window.

The only piece of furniture in the vast room was a modern black leather sofa with aluminium legs, standing in the centre of the space, facing the window. Marcia was just passing it when she heard the familiar whirr of a sliding door. She span round. None of the three doors behind her were opening. The whirr emanated from that other corridor.

Now she could hear a woman's voice: 'This isn't good enough, Dr Marmwell. You've been avoiding us. How much longer are we to be kept waiting?'

It was a voice Marcia knew well. The voice of her mother. Footsteps. Coming towards the room. Marcia rushed to the sofa, threw herself onto it and lay along the three seats, concealed by the high back.

A man's voice: 'Alicia, I can assure you that you won't have to wait for much longer. And please, call me Gerald.'

Her father's voice: 'We were promised Marcia's treatment would begin immediately, Dr Marmwell. We brought the five hundred thousand. Cash, like you asked for. I demand that you honour your side of the arrangement.'

'Alicia, Marcus, believe me, everything is proceeding as we agreed. Relax. Take a seat on the sofa and we can discuss your concerns calmly.'

Trapped! No, quick – roll off the front of the sofa. Now roll back under it. Squeeze under. Did they see me? Can they see me now? No. They're still talking.

'Finest view in the Arctic. I often sit here to get inspiration.'

The Arctic! Keep still. Here they come. Mum's shoes. Dad's shoes. Man's shoes. *Ow!* Marcia managed to keep silent as her already cramped hiding place was squashed even smaller by three people sitting down.

Her mother's voice again: 'Same damn view as the one from that room you're keeping us in.'

'You're not being kept anywhere, Alicia. The whole of our Deluxe Hospitality Wing is yours to enjoy. The sauna, the Jacuzzi, the DVD cinema suite.'

'So why can't we leave the hospitality wing? Why all the guards? The locks on the doors?'

'Marcus, you and Alicia are simply being chaperoned for your own protection. Your personal safety during your stay here at Nordbergen Research Enterprises is of paramount concern to us. And you couldn't possibly leave the building. It's minus forty-five degrees out there.'

'I demand that you give us back our mobile phones. I'm going to call our lawyer.'

'Alicia, we made it absolutely clear to you when we met

in London how vital secrecy was to our work here – for your benefit and ours. Mobile phones contravene our strict communications policy. They'll be returned to you on your homeward flight. Look, I can see you're stressed. Why don't you both go and give yourselves a good workout in the gym? Works for me every time.'

'Damn it, Marmwell, we didn't come to this godforsaken island to play on exercise machines. We came here to get our daughter sorted out. When is the treatment going to start?'

'Tomorrow, Marcus. I promise. As soon as Professor Murdo returns from his business trip tomorrow morning, he'll begin work on your daughter.'

'And this treatment really will work?'

'Marcus, we went through all this in London. Professor Murdo is the world's leading specialist in the field of Human Genetic Modification. He will eradicate Marcia's unwanted genetic components and replace them with carefully selected genes taken from yourselves; the genes you would have chosen to pass on to Marcia had this technology been available when you conceived her. Genes which will make her intelligent, outgoing, sophisticated, obedient, hardworking and ambitious. Professor Murdo will then perform extensive cosmetic surgery to give Marcia a face and physique to match her new genetic identity; the face and physique she would have developed if she'd inherited the right genes from you from the outset. Lastly, Professor Murdo will use laser-surgery on a very specific section of the memory cells in Marcia's brain. Once her operation scars have healed and we bring her back to full consciousness, she'll have no recollection of her former personality or appearance. The upbringing and education you have given her will remain intact, of course, but she will now have the genes to enable her to appreciate everything you've lavished on her. She'll never know anything about the treatment – we'll simply tell her she's been in hospital following a car accident – but *you'll* know that you've given your daughter the greatest gift of all: the right genes. Not any old genes, passed on at random; but your very *best* genes, carefully selected and lovingly gifted to her. Just think – in less than two months' time, you'll be able to return to London with the perfect daughter you deserve. Surely that's worth waiting one more day for?'

Chapter Twenty-Four

Marcia felt sick and numb.

A pause. Then her father's voice: 'Well, if you're *sure* the treatment will begin tomorrow.'

'I promise,' said Dr Marmwell. 'The couple of days she's spent under sedation have been an ideal preparation for her treatment.'

'As long as you've got her under twenty-four-hour surveillance,' said her mother, as the three of them stood up and began to move back across the room. 'She can be a devious little urchin.'

Biting her lip with anger, Marcia turned her head to watch them walk away – first she could just see their feet and ankles, then their legs and bodies. She couldn't see their heads from her position under the sofa. Did that mean *they* wouldn't see *her* if they turned round?

'Marcia is being monitored at regular intervals,' said Dr Marmwell. 'I assure you that right now she's sleeping soundly in a room from which she can't possibly escape.'

From his voice, Marcia was pretty sure that Dr Marmwell was the man who had come into her room with the woman yesterday. His legs and her parents' legs were joined by another pair, clad in black trousers and boots.

'Ah, Kurt,' said Dr Marmwell. 'Perhaps you could escort Mr and Mrs Slick to the gymnasium and see that everything is set up to their satisfaction. See you later,' he called, as Marcia's parents were taken back into the Deluxe Hospitality Wing. 'And relax! Everything's going to be fine.'

Marcia felt her head burning inside. It was worse than she had imagined. What her parents were planning was as bad as killing her. No, worse. They were going to kill everything that was herself, then use her empty body; fill it with their own idea of a perfect daughter and pretend it was still her. Why did they hate her so much the way she was? What was wrong with her? No. She mustn't think like that. It was her parents who were wrong. She wouldn't let them do this. She was going to escape. But how?

Dr Marmwell was still there. Marcia watched him walk to one of the three steel doors in the veneered wall, the one on the right. As he reached it, the door on the left slid open and a grey plastic wheelie bin came rolling through. The bin was being pushed, Marcia could just make out, by a man in dark green overalls.

'Ah, Steve,' said Dr Marmwell. 'You taking the office waste down in the lift? Take a trolley of empty bottles from the lab too, will you? It's just in here.'

Leaving the wheelie bin next to the middle door, which Marcia guessed must be the lift, Steve followed Dr Marmwell through the right-hand door. It closed behind them.

This was it! It might be her only chance.  Quick, out from under the sofa, across the carpet. No one in either corridor. Open the wheelie bin. Half full of screwed up paper and plastic coffee cups. Clamber up. Careful! Don't tip it over. Get in. Lid down. Dark. Stinks of old ashtrays. Doesn't matter. Could be worse. Sit still. Don't let the paper rustle.

Whirr. The lab door opening. Rattling glass on the trolley. Whirr. Lift door opening. Oof! Bin tipping back on wheels. Will he notice the extra weight? Moving. Clunk. Upright again. Now the rattling trolley. Lift door whirring shut. Going down. Where to? To be tipped out and discovered? To be wheeled outside? How long could you survive at minus forty-five degrees in a pair of pyjamas?

Bump. The lift's stopped. Whirr. Getting out? No, the bin's not moving. Rumbling of wheels. Someone else getting in?

'All right, Gary? That the last of the bins from the canteen?'

'Yeah, that's the lot, Steve.'

Whirr. Going down again.

'I hate it here. They said I was gonna be part of a security force. Snowmobiles, guns 'n' stuff. All I've done is clean toilets. And now you've got me taking bins out. Could've done that if I'd stayed at my mum's.'

'Shut it, Gary.'

'They won't even let me phone my mum; tell her where I am.'

'Shut it! Or I'll report you to Smedling.'

Silence.

Bump. Stopped again. Whirr. Rumbling: Gary's bin out first. Rattling: trolley out. Bin tipping back again. Rolling. Clunk. Upright. Haven't gone far.

'Right, snowsuits on.'

Footsteps. Have they gone? Push up the lid and look. Just a few millimetres. Can't see much. Small room. The tops of six more wheelie bins. The top of the bottle trolley. Double doors with small tinted windows. An open doorway over there. Is that where the men went? What's that sound? Zips. And a swishing noise. Waterproof clothing. They're coming back. Lid down.

'Get a bin and follow me. They've all gotta go out to the incinerator.'

An incinerator! *Don't take this bin. Don't take this bin.* Clunk. Not my bin. Clunk. Not my bin either. Whirr. Must be those double doors opening. Rumbling wheels and footsteps. Whirr. The doors must close automatically.

Quick. Get out, before they come back. Steady. Feet up and over. Jump down. Brush paper off pyjamas. Put it back in bin. What's through that open doorway? Can't hear anyone. Peep round. A changing room. Snowsuits on hooks, snow boots on the bench underneath. No one about. Now, the double doors – see where the men are going.

Marcia crept to the double doors and looked through one of the tinted windows. Steve and Gary, clad in hooded black snowsuits, were pushing the wheelie bins along a short passageway, towards two armed guards who stood by another set of doors. Marcia saw Steve hold up a laminated card whilst continuing to push his bin with his other hand. One guard gave a nod and pressed a panel on the wall. The doors slid open and Steve and Gary passed out into daylight.

A sudden realization sent a tingle up Marcia's spine. Gary had needed no security pass of his own. He had simply walked out behind Steve. Dare she attempt the reckless plan that was forming in her mind?

Chapter Twenty-Five

'Pressure ridge,' said Yuri, pointing ahead. His prediction that the ice might become more difficult had proved correct. By midmorning they had begun to encounter more and more ice rubble and now they had come up against this four-metre-high barrier: a wall of broken blocks of white ice that stretched away to either side as far as the eye could see.

'No way round. We will have to go over,' said Yuri, scanning the ridge for the least steep section.

'What makes the ice pile up like that?' asked Zara as they approached the obstacle.

'Pressure ridge is formed by one section of ice crashing into other,' explained Yuri. 'The ice is changing all the time. This is an ocean, remember. Big tides, powerful currents, even when surface is freezed.'

'It's weird to think that we're not travelling over solid land,' said Sam. 'That all this is moving.'

'Weird, yes,' agreed Yuri. The ski-boat tilted back as he revved onto the foot of the slope. 'Weird and dangerous.'

For the next ten minutes no one spoke, as Yuri wrestled with the ski-boat through a jerky, jinking course up the uneven blocks. The engine growled and grumbled until eventually they made it to the top.

They looked down over a daunting view: a chaotic labyrinth of massive ice blocks and deep ice gullies. It looked to Zara like the wreckage of some enormous smashed meringue. 'Now what?' she said. 'We'll never be able to drive through that.'

'We will find a way,' said Yuri. 'Maybe we can use leads.'

'Leads?' echoed Sam. 'You mean electric cables?'

'No. Leads of water between ice, where it has pulled apart.' Yuri was pointing at a flat dark ribbon that zigzagged between the white ice rubble. 'That lead has already frozen over. Smoother for us, if course is right.' He turned to Ben. 'What d'you reckon, navigator?'

'It'd take us *almost* in the right direction,' said Ben, chuffed to be consulted. 'Looks more north-north-west than north-west but we could compensate later.'

'Righty-ho then,' said Yuri, easing the ski-boat forward. Once more, conversation ceased, to allow Yuri to concentrate. Having finally completed the steep, jolting descent, the ski-boat had to struggle over another hundred metres of ice rubble to reach the nearest part of the lead.

The children could see that the surface of the lead was indeed frozen over, with an almost transparent layer of brown ice. As they drove on to it, the ice sagged beneath their weight, then bounced back as they zoomed along, as if it were a layer of rubber. Surely ice was brittle. It couldn't be bendy, could it?

'Sea water freeze very different to fresh water,' laughed Yuri, seeing their surprised expressions. 'This is young ice. Won't support us for long.' The ice confirmed his opinion by creaking then shattering beneath them. The children clung to the edges of their seats as ice and water splashed up over the cab's windows but Yuri simply grinned and pulled two levers beside the steering wheel. 'Skis retracted . . . propeller engaged . . . There!' The ski-boat motored forward, easily ploughing a course through the lead's semi-frozen surface.

'In ordinary snowmobile, to fall in water is very dangerous. We would all be dead,' remarked Yuri cheerfully. 'A fine mess. You are better off in amphibious machine like this, yes?'

'Definitely,' agreed Zara. Although it was warm now in the well-heated cab, the sight of the icy bow wave churning past the windows made her shiver.

Chapter Twenty-Six

Five minutes had passed before Steve and Gary returned with their empty bins. Steve took the bottle trolley. Gary took another wheelie bin. Neither man so much as glanced into the changing room. Neither man noticed that one of the black snowsuits was not actually hanging from a hook, but was standing on the bench, facing the wall. Neither man, passing back through the double doors, saw the snowsuit step down from the bench, tiptoe into the room, quietly take the nearest of the remaining bins and roll it after them.

This is mad, fretted Marcia, just making it through the closing doors. Surely they can hear me? Maybe not, with their hoods up and with the noise of the other bin and the bottle trolley. But what if Steve turns round to talk to Gary? And what about the guards? They'll realize they've never seen me before, even with my hood up over my face like this. They'll say something to Steve about his extra assistant. They'll . . . Calm down. Don't panic. Keep footsteps in pace with Gary. But walk normally. Head down. Don't look guilty, look bored. Think bored. Just taking the bins out. Supposed to be here. Don't bother looking at me.

Steve showing his security pass. Guard opening doors. Steve through. Gary through. Other guard looking at me. Don't look back at him. Head down . . . Keep going . . . *Through!*

The cold hit Marcia with a brutal intensity. She had put on two snowsuits, the smallest one she could find worn under a bigger one, both zipped right up over her nose. Now she wished she'd put on three. She wore the overlong legs of the outer snowsuit down over her feet, in place of socks, inside the oversized snow boots, and wore both pairs of gloves she'd found, yet her toes and fingers were gripped by pain within seconds of stepping outside.

Fighting down her instinct to move quickly and warm herself up, Marcia walked steadily behind Steve and Gary down a ridged rubber pathway leading directly away from the doors. The pathway ran between two curved extensions whose smooth silvery sides were too high to see over. What kind of building had she been in? She mustn't look behind her. Look ahead. Low grey outbuildings. The frozen sea beyond.

Any second now, one of the guards would shout for her to stop; aim his machine gun and . . . *Clunk!* A noise behind her! Calm down. Not a gun. The doors closing. Keep walking.

Beyond the ends of the strange metallic extensions, the path joined another track in a T-junction. This track was curved and, from its arc, Marcia guessed that it encircled the building, though she still dared not turn round to check. The outbuildings she had seen fringed the outer rim of the track; concrete huts, raised Portakabins and a large corrugated-metal building which looked as if it might be an aircraft hangar.

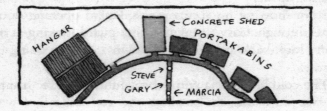

Steve turned left. He'd see her! No, his hood was blocking his peripheral vision. Gary turned left. Should she follow? No. This was her chance.

Straight on, across the new track, off the edge. Don't slip! Into the narrow gap between that concrete shed and that Portakabin. Are the guards still watching? Keep going. Turn right, behind the Portakabin. Made it. No one back here – just snow and rocks down to the ice.

Cold! So so cold. Everything hurts. Feel faint. Starving. Need food. Need food or I'll die. The wheelie bin. Is it one of the bins from the canteen? Open it . . . Yes! Food!

Marcia plunged her gloved hands into the bin and crammed pieces of leftover food into her mouth. Bits of pork pie, scrapings of rice and mashed potato, bacon fat, half-eaten fried eggs, crusts of bread – anything. The food at the top of the bin didn't smell rotten, though she wouldn't have been able to stop herself eating it if it had. Her body craved food, the fattier the better. She ate and ate until at last she felt her insides coming back to life again, her strength returning.

Then she jumped up and down on the spot, flinging her hands out, slapping her arms; anything to bring some warmth back to her limbs.

She stopped suddenly. A trundling noise. Steve and Gary coming back. Had she left footprints? Would they stop and . . . No. They were gone.

Marcia got back to her feet and stumbled along the back of the Portakabin. She wanted to see what kind of building she'd been imprisoned in. From the high position of that large room and from the length of the corridors, she knew it must be enormous. She reached the corner and peeped round.

Marcia stared. She stared and stared in absolute astonishment.

Chapter Twenty-Seven

'Yuri to Frank . . . Come in, Frank . . . Are you receiving me? Over.'

'Frank to Yuri,' crackled Frank's voice. 'Receiving you loud and clear. Please give your current position. Over.'

Yuri gave a nod to Sam, who was now taking a turn in the front.

'Seventy-three degrees five minutes north; thirty-six degrees eleven minutes east,' read Sam from the GPS. 'Er . . . over.'

'Got that. Seventy-three degrees five minutes north; thirty six degrees eleven minutes east. You're making good progress. Over.'

'Yes indeedy,' said Yuri. 'All dandy and fine with us. We've just had luncheon.'

It hadn't taken long that morning for their lead to freeze over properly and for two hours their vehicle had sped effortlessly along its frosted white surface. By lunchtime, Zara had calculated they were halfway there, though the lead had then started to veer too far north and they had abandoned it. Now they were back on the pack-ice, steering a meandering course between high clusters of ice rubble.

'Have you been able to contact Olaf?' continued Yuri. 'Over.'

'Afraid not,' reported Frank. 'Still nothing at all. Over.'

'Never mind,' said Yuri. 'We will be there soon anyway. Over.'

'I hope so. The weather's worsening back here. Snowstorm approaching from the east. Over.'

'Don't you worry. We will be sitting in Bjørn's Bar with Olaf long before the storm catches us,' declared Yuri. 'Over and out.'

'Take care. Over and out.'

Over the next half-hour, the ice rubble increased, their detours widened and their progress slowed. 'Don't worry,' said Yuri. 'Probably this is last obstruction now, then we get good straight run.'

They rounded the pile of rubble. No one spoke. A few hundred metres ahead, a monstrous pressure ridge lay directly across their course. It was at least twelve metres tall; higher than a house.

Yuri shrugged. 'We got over little one. We can get over big one.' He revved the engine and sped towards the ridge, his lips fixed in a confident smile.

Only once did Sam notice an anxious frown flash across the old man's face, not when Yuri was looking at the pressure ridge but when he glanced into his wing mirror. Sam looked round. Behind them, to the east, the sky was turning a strange shade of browny-grey. Above the southern horizon, the sun still shone, but it looked redder than it had before and its light had taken on a hazier quality.

'Is the snowstorm coming?' Sam asked.

'We will beat it, easy-peasy,' said Yuri. Ben and Zara turned to look at the sky and Sam wished he hadn't spoken.

The pressure ridge loomed above them, its almost vertical cliff of ice boulders defying their little craft to even attempt an ascent. Undaunted, Yuri slammed the accelerator pedal to the floor and vroomed the ski-boat onto the lowest blocks.

The vehicle tipped up at a terrifying angle, pressing the children back into their seats. Yuri twisted the wheel this way and that, struggling to find a route from one boulder to the next. Many times the front skis jammed in the ice rubble. Many times the drive belt lost contact with the ice, causing the engine to rev wildly. Many times they slithered back helplessly as Yuri fought to regain control. But somehow Yuri forced the machine on, doggedly gaining two metres for every metre lost, until, with a final furious roar, the ski-boat lumbered onto the top of the ridge.

'There! Perfect ice!' cried Yuri, sounding immensely relieved. From their high viewpoint they could see flat white ice stretching all the way to the horizon, with only a few easily avoidable obstacles. 'Now we go speedy. We will beat storm, no problem.'

But before they had time to begin their descent, the ridge shuddered below them with an unearthly rumble. A few metres away, two ice boulders wobbled, then tumbled from the top of the ridge, smashing as they fell.

'Ice is moving!' Yuri shouted. 'We must drive off ridge fast!'

The ski-boat lurched into its descent, pitching them forward against their seat belts. Yuri nursed the vehicle through a winding course off the uppermost boulders. He was heading towards a great slab of white ice, which formed a natural ramp down. Before they could reach it, the ridge shook once more, again with that eerie, graunching rumble, louder than before. Blocks of ice were shifting and tumbling all around them. Then the block they were driving over seemed to kick up beneath them. The children screamed as  the ski-boat somersaulted into thin air. The world rolled and span chaotically past the windows.

BANG. Their screams were cut short as the ski-boat ricocheted off a boulder and the seat belts jolted the air from their lungs. But still they tumbled down.

BANG . . . BANG . . . BANG . . .

Three more times they hit the ice, until their violent fall ended in a terrible, deafening *CRASH!*

Chapter Twenty-Eight

Not a sound but the howling of the wind outside. No engine.

Zara's voice: 'Is everyone all right?'

Sam felt his forehead. Sore but no blood. Just a bump where the GPS had bounced off him during the fall. Aching ribs under the tight seat belt.

'I'm all right,' he croaked, though he felt terribly shaken. Disorientated. The pull of gravity felt at odds with the cab's interior. The ski-boat had landed on the driver's side. Sam looked down at Yuri.

Yuri! Lifeless. Eyes shut. Body held by seat belt but head lying on the smashed side window. Blood trickling over shards of glass and onto the hard white ice beneath.

Ben's voice: '*I'm* all right. But Yuri . . .'

Zara gasped as she looked at the old man. 'Is he dead?' she cried. He couldn't be dead. Not Yuri. Was this what her mum and dad had looked like?

'He might not be,' said Ben. 'Quick!'

Jolting themselves out of their paralysing state of shock, the three children unfastened their seat belts and clambered awkwardly down the cab's interior. Sam tried to find a pulse on Yuri's wrist as Ben lifted his head.

Suddenly they could hear Yuri breathing. Sickly, rasping breathing but a beautiful sound to them. With an effort, they undid Yuri's seat belt and sat his inert body on the inside of the driver's door, which was now their floor. The side of his head was a sticky mess of blood and glass.

'Yuri!' said Zara, loudly. 'Can you hear us?' No response.

'First-aid kit,' said Sam, rummaging vainly through the tumbled junk in the glove compartment.

'Here!' said Zara, finding a white box marked with a red cross under Yuri's seat. 'We must stop the bleeding.'

'We've gotta clean all the glass out first,' said Ben, remembering bits of a swimming-club first-aid course.

It took some time to pick and swab all the glass out. Although there was a lot of blood, there was no big open wound. Clearly Yuri had been knocked out by the craggy, icy surface as it smashed through the window on impact.

'The blood's clotting up anyway,' said Zara, as they bandaged Yuri's head. 'Maybe we should have let the air get to it.'

'I reckon it's *freezing* up,' said Ben. 'The heater's packed up along with the engine. Better put his balaclava and hood on or the wound'll get frostbitten.'

'Yuri, wake up!' implored Zara, desperately. Still no response. It was all such a mess. What should they do? She tried to think logically. One thing at a time. 'We've got to get the ski-boat upright first,' she decided. 'Then we can lay Yuri on the back seat. Strap him back into his seat for now.'

'Full kit on,' Ben reminded them. The cold was already beginning to bite. The children struggled up through the other side door and slithered down the cab roof onto the ice. They stumbled round the vehicle, surveying the damage. The hull, though badly dented, seemed intact, and the skis looked OK. But at the back of the ski-boat they were confronted by a grim sight: the engine and drive belt were a smashed and mangled mess, clearly beyond any repair they could attempt.

'Come on; ski-boat upright first,' insisted Zara. They all pushed against the cab roof but the ski-boat remained stuck on its side.

'We need something to lever it,' said Sam, trying to unlace one corner of tarpaulin without spilling the entire load.

It took twenty minutes of levering with ice axes and pulling with ropes before they finally succeeded in rolling and jolting the ski-boat back onto its four skis. 'Back in the cab,' puffed Zara. They were all exhausted.

'We should bring in that crate of food,' said Ben, remembering something he'd read about polar exploration. 'When it's this cold, you have to eat tons.'

Yuri didn't seem any worse, in spite of the further jolting, and they laid him down on the back seat. Then they each ate three bars of chocolate without pausing.

'Next thing is to block up this broken window before we freeze to death,' said Zara, shivering. 'Especially as we can't get the heater going with the engine bust.'

'And we should radio Frank,' said Ben, flicking the switch on the dashboard. Nothing. Not even a hiss.

'Must've broken inside when we crashed,' concluded Sam, after they'd tried every switch they could find. 'I don't know anything about fixing radios. But I reckon it's worth looking at the heater.' He crouched down onto the floor and under the dashboard. 'It might run separately from the engine . . . There's a big battery under here. I think some wires have broken loose. Let's get the tool box from the back.'

Fifteen minutes later, Zara and Ben had managed to jam a roughly sawn section of the food crate lid into the window frame.

'How are you doing, Sam?' enquired Zara, as she sealed up the edges with heavy-duty tape.

'Just twisting together the last two wires,' said Sam. 'If I plug this back into the battery, it might . . .'

Wshhhhh.

'You've done it!' exclaimed Zara, holding her gloved hands in the hot air. 'Sam, you're a genius!'

'I'm not sure how long the battery will last without the engine recharging it,' said Sam. 'Let's hope it lasts out till someone rescues us. Maybe when Frank doesn't hear from us he'll —'

'But it'll be too late!' interrupted Ben. 'Even if we *are* rescued, it'll be too late to save Uncle Alexander.'

The low sun had long since been obliterated from view. Thick browny-grey clouds loomed over the pressure ridge. The snowstorm could not be far off now.

'There must be *something* we can do!' fretted Zara. 'If I thought it would help Uncle Alexander, I'd start *walking* to Petrøya. But it would be pointless. We couldn't walk five miles out there, especially in this wind.'

'That's it!' yelled Ben. 'The wind! Look.' Ignoring Sam and Zara's puzzled faces, he wrestled the drive-belt lever up until something went clunk at the back of the vehicle. With nothing to anchor the ski-boat against the easterly wind, it slithered slowly westward across the ice. 'See?' cried Ben, lowering the drive belt to brake them once more. 'It moved! Only slowly and not quite in the right direction, but if we had a *sail* . . .'

'You're right!' said Sam, enthusiastically. 'We can turn the ski-boat into an ice yacht!'

'The tarpaulin cover!' said Zara. 'That'd make a square sail, like on a Viking ship.'

'We'll have to make a mast strong enough to hold up a big crossbar,' said Ben. 'And I'm not sure how well it will steer.'

'Two triangular sails might be better,' Sam suggested. 'I've only been sailing once but that's what all the dinghies

had. Like this . . .' He pulled his notebook and a pen out of
his rucksack and started scribbling a rough diagram.

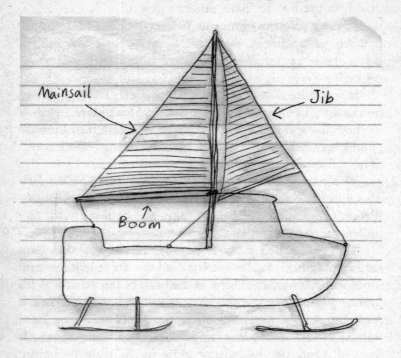

'See, you have a mainsail at the back, with a boom along
the bottom, fixed to the mast down here. Then the jib sail
at the front, like this. You can get anywhere you want by
tacking or gybing. I *think* I can remember how it works.'

'Looks good to me,' said Zara.

For the next hour and a half, hampered by the wind, the
cold and their cumbersome gloves, they worked harder
than any of them had worked in their lives.

First they clambered onto the tarpaulin cover and sliced
it from corner to corner with a knife, making two triangular

sails. Next they lashed every piece of straight, long equipment they had into a three-metre mast and a two metre
boom. They used the skis and ski poles, the ice axes and
shovel, timber from broken-up crates, and even Yuri's
unloaded gun. What the mast and boom lacked in elegance,
they made up for in strength.

They fastened the mast to a built-in metal ladder on the
back of the cab and secured it with rigging lines. Fixing the
boom and sails in place proved almost impossible in the
increasingly high wind but, by furling the sails, they eventually succeeded.

Lastly, they tied a long rope to the end of the boom and
another two to the bottom corner of the jib. 'These ropes
are to control the sails,' explained Sam. 'I *think* they're called
sheets.'

By now, the children were shattered; every thought,
every action made sluggish by the numbing cold. Yet
nothing could dampen their sense of achievement as
they completed their sturdy-looking ice yacht.

'Two of us'll need to stay out here and pull the sails tight
as we set off,' said Sam, looping the sheet ropes ready
around various metal fittings. 'One of us needs to be at the
wheel to steer.'

'You go in and drive, Zara,' said Ben. 'You're the eldest.
Me and Sam'll climb in through the other side door once
we're going.'

'All right,' agreed Zara. 'But let's hurry! Here comes the
blizzard.'

Already, flakes of snow were swirling in on the wind.
Above the pressure ridge, they could see a mass of white
specks, seething and rolling within the storm cloud.

'Ready!' shouted Sam, as Zara got into the cab. 'Lift the
drive belt!'

The drive belt graunched up. Sam and Ben unfurled the sails and hauled on the sheets.

Whump! Whump!

Both sails filled out instantly, tarpaulin stretched in taut curves, and the ice yacht zoomed forward so fast that Sam nearly fell backwards. As he and Ben hitched the sheets secure, they whooped and cheered. They were on their way again at last, racing along with the storm biting at their heels.

Chapter Twenty-Nine

'She sails pretty well!' yelled Ben proudly.

'Yep,' answered Sam, reasonably sure that everything was standing up to the strain. 'Let's get in.'

Taking great care, Ben and Sam managed the perilous climb round the outside of the cab. They opened the passenger door and swung themselves in. Zara was leaning forward over the big steering wheel, lips tight with concentration.

'Better check our course,' said Ben. 'Where's the GPS?'

'I haven't seen it since it we crashed,' said Sam, joining Ben on the floor to look for it.

'Here it is,' said Ben. 'We'll need to plug it back into the – Oh.'

He brought the device up from under the seat. The screen was shattered.

'I should've held on to it,' lamented Sam.

'Not your fault,' said Ben. 'Anyway, we've got our compasses. Let's have that map with our last position on and I'll work out the bearing for Petrøya. Steer west–north-west for now.'

'But we can't stay on one bearing all the way,' Zara pointed out. 'We'll have to go round ice blocks and rubble.'

'As long as we mark each detour on the map, we'll still know where we are,' said Ben.

'Only if we know our speed and mileage,' Zara said. 'But the speedometer and milometer aren't working now.'

'We'll just have to guess our speed,' said Ben, 'and time everything carefully. It won't be perfect but we should be pretty close.'

'OK,' agreed Zara. 'You're the expert.'

Actually Ben was feeling nothing like as confident as he sounded. He felt lost without the comforting GPS. Although he was pretty good with a compass, he knew that even a tiny deviation could result in them completely missing a small island a hundred and twenty miles away.

'Ice boulders ahead!' shouted Zara.

'We'll go round to the south of them,' said Ben. 'Steer left.'

A thought struck Sam. 'The sails'll need to come across,' he said.

He and Ben climbed out and tumbled into the open back section once more. Behind them, the pressure ridge had been swallowed up by the blizzard. Visibility was better ahead for the time being but the snowstorm was definitely catching up with them.

Sam tried to recall the right scrap of information from his very limited sailing knowledge. He was pretty sure that to change tack with the wind behind you was called gybing. He was also pretty sure that beginners weren't supposed to attempt it but he tried to put that out of his mind.

'You take the jib sheets, Ben,' he yelled. 'I'll do the main sheet.'

On their current west-north-west course, the easterly wind was blowing the sails out to port, or left. Zara steered left and for a moment the wind was dead behind them. As she veered further towards their new south-west course, the jib sail began to flap and Ben adjusted the two sheets to let it flip across.

Sam hauled the boom in to the middle of the boat, keeping his head low as it passed over. The mainsail slackened for a second, then filled with wind from the other side and Sam carefully let it billow out to starboard.

Ben raised a thumb. They had done it! Their ice yacht really worked.

They quickly passed the stretch of ice boulders, and a pan of smooth ice opened up to their right.

'Steer back onto west-north-west,' shouted Ben, hammering on the cab roof.

As Zara steered once more, Ben loosened off the jib. But before Sam had even touched the main sheet, the boom and mainsail flew across at lightning speed. The boom cracked his head, the ice yacht tipped and Sam felt himself going over the port side. Crying out, he grasped a trailing rope with one hand and just managed to flail one foot back over the edge. The ice yacht hurtled onwards, balanced on its left-hand skis. Ice raced past beneath him, inches from his face. Mustn't let go. Zara and Ben might never find him in the blizzard. Strength going in fingers . . . losing grip . . . slipping . . .

Just in time, Sam felt a hand grab his hood and haul him back to safety. 'Thanks, Ben,' he croaked, as the ice yacht dropped back onto all four skis.

Ben sheeted in the flapping jib and helped Sam back into the cab.

'I'm really sorry, Sam,' said Zara. 'I think I steered too sharply.'

Sam shook his head. 'No – my fault. But we'd better wear safety lines outside from now on.'

Their diversion had cost them their narrow lead on the storm and the blizzard soon overtook them. Snow covered the back window within minutes and though the front windscreen remained just about clear, they could barely see thirty metres ahead.

Onwards they hurtled, swept along by the relentless wind, battling to stave off disaster as the hours passed;

Zara straining to see ahead, hands gripped to the wheel, swerving round obstacles almost before her brain had registered them; Ben and Sam struggling out into the blizzard to work sails they could hardly see with hands that could hardly feel; Ben's brain wrestling all the while with bearings and calculations; Sam's eyes constantly checking for the next section of mast or boom to need a running repair; all of them fighting off collapse with a constant intake of food, the boys feeding Zara at the wheel.

Yuri continued to lie on the back seat, breathing but showing no sign of regaining consciousness.

Late afternoon darkened to early evening, adding to the desolate feeling of being alone in the middle of nowhere. Ben switched on the headlamp, an adjustable light on the front of the cab roof, which had miraculously survived the crash.

'We *ought* to be nearly there by now,' said Ben, studying his zigzag of pen lines and numbers which marked their estimated progress across the map. 'But maybe we've not been going as fast as I've been guessing. Or maybe our diversions have been wider than I've marked.'

Or maybe we've gone completely off course and we're heading for Greenland, all three of them were thinking. But nobody said it. They sailed on for another twenty minutes, cheering each other up by wondering if the blizzard was easing off a little.

The headlamp flickered and dimmed. 'Battery must be going,' said Sam. The *wshhhhh* of the heater dropped in tone, confirming this. It was obvious that neither appliance would keep going much longer.

The blizzard *was* easing off. For minutes at a time, the wind, fortunately as strong as ever, became relatively snow-free.

'A light!' cried Sam suddenly.

'*Where?*' shouted Zara.

'Are you sure?' asked Ben.

'Yes! It was over there, flashing. To the right, ahead of us – there it is again!'

This time they all saw it. A distant white light, flashing twice.

'It's gone again,' said Zara.

'It must be a lighthouse!' said Ben. 'Flashing every ten seconds or so. It must be land!'

They peered into the gloom, waiting for the light to reappear but, suddenly, a flurry of snow closed in, obscuring everything.

'Doesn't matter,' said Ben. 'I got a bearing. Steer north-north-west.'

After a long ten minutes, the snow cleared again. There was the light, flashing twice, dead ahead of them now, much nearer. And they could see more lights, clustered near the lighthouse beacon.

'It *has* to be Petrøya!' shouted Zara. 'We've done it! . . . *We've done it!*'

Tears of relief rolled down her cheeks. Ben hugged Sam; Sam hugged Ben; they both hugged Zara, who had to make herself keep both hands on the wheel.

Sam got his binoculars out. He could just make out the various lamps and lighted windows of what looked like a tiny harbour village. 'There's a neon sign on one of the buildings,' he said, trying to keep the binoculars steady as the ice yacht rattled along. 'I can't quite read it . . . Hang on . . . Yes! It says Bjørn's Bar!'

Chapter Thirty

Soon their little craft was speeding into Petrøya's frozen harbour. Bjørn's Bar stood directly ahead, in a row of timber buildings behind the quay.

Sam and Ben were out on the back. Sam waited until Zara had steered safely through the narrow gap in the high harbour wall before shouting 'Now!'

Together, the boys unhitched the sheets. The released mainsail and boom blew round to join the flapping jib at the front but, even without power, the ice yacht continued to slide across the smooth harbour ice towards the inner wall.

'Zara! Put down the drive belt!' yelled Ben.

'I'm trying to!' came Zara's voice from the cab. 'It's stuck.' She swerved to avoid crashing head on.

CRRRRUNCH. Metal graunching against stone, the ice yacht scraped, spun and clattered to a halt against the harbour steps.

Sam and Ben sat where they had fallen by the foot of the mast. Zara released the wheel and flopped back in her seat. Though unscathed by their bumpy arrival, the three children were finally overcome by exhaustion.

Then there were voices. Footsteps. Ben staggered to his feet to see people hurrying down the steps. 'We need help!' he called. 'We've come here with Yuri, from Barents Ter– from Frank and Yuri's old weather station. He's injured. Unconscious, on the back seat.'

Then many hands were half-guiding, half-lifting the children up the steps. Ben looked back to see Yuri, wrapped in furs, being carried on a makeshift stretcher.

In less than a minute, they found themselves bustled into the bar and into chairs by a blazing fire. Someone pressed bowls of hot soup into their hands. As warmth and strength returned to their bodies, a dozen adults talked at once; asking questions, congratulating them for constructing the mast and sails, and for having navigated so far through the blizzard.

'Please, listen!' said Zara loudly, and the room fell hushed. 'First,' she continued, 'is Yuri all right? Is he going to be OK?'

'I think so,' said a large blond man, in a strong Norwegian accent. 'We have no permanent doctor on the island but one of my customers has a little medical knowledge. He is taking a look at Yuri now, upstairs. I am Bjørn. This is my bar. What brings you to Petrøya?'

'We need to speak to Olaf Nansen,' said Zara. 'It's urgent. We tried to radio him from Frank and Yuri's but we couldn't get through.'

'All the radios and telephones on Petrøya have been out of order for several days,' said Bjørn. 'Even mobiles. We do not know why. But if it is Olaf you have come all this way to see, I have bad news. Olaf disappeared two weeks ago.'

'*Disappeared?*' exclaimed Ben. 'What do you mean? Where to?'

'We do not know,' sighed Bjørn. 'We have been searching everywhere. On the island, on the ice. But no trace of Olaf or of his snowmobile. We are worried he has been attacked by a bear and . . .'

'We must not give up hope,' a voice interrupted. Everyone turned to see a tall, good-looking man enter the room. He wore a dark blue snowsuit, boots, gloves and a peaked cap.

'This is Officer Ormstad,' Bjørn told the children. 'Olaf's replacement from Norway.'

'*Temporary* replacement, I hope,' Officer Ormstad said, smiling. 'I'm sure we will find Officer Nansen safe and well. Of course, our efforts are not helped by this wretched communications blackout. I hope to get that situation remedied very soon.'

'I hope so,' said Bjørn. 'If the radios were working, these children would have been saved a four-hundred-kilometre journey.'

'That's a long way,' said Officer Ormstad to the children, looking impressed. 'What has brought you to Petrøya? Where have you come from?'

'We came to find Officer Nansen,' explained Zara, concentrating hard on telling everything clearly. She had to make Olaf's replacement believe them and take action. 'We needed him to organize a rescue mission to Nordbergen. Our uncle . . .'

'Wait,' interrupted Officer Ormstad. 'This sounds like a real crisis. You had better come to my office in the police station. You can tell me everything properly there.'

'They've only just arrived!' protested Bjørn. 'They are frozen and exhausted.'

'It is only next door,' insisted Officer Ormstad. 'If this is an emergency, it must be dealt with correctly.'

'It's OK,' agreed Zara, relieved that Officer Ormstad was taking them so seriously. 'It *is* urgent,' she told Bjørn.

'Well, don't be long,' said Bjørn. 'I will keep your soup warm.'

The children followed Officer Ormstad outside and into the grey-painted building next door. He ushered them into a tidy office, found them each a chair and sat down behind his desk. 'Now then,' he said, picking up a pen and notebook. 'What's all this about Nordbergen?'

Sam sat back in his chair. Zara could do the talking. At last they had found someone with the authority to organize a full-scale rescue. Then something caught his eye. Something which sent a terrible shudder through his insides. Behind Officer Ormstad stood a metal locker. The door was ajar and, inside, Sam could just see a black combat jacket hanging up. The shoulder of the jacket's right sleeve bore a small emblem: the black silhouette of a raven's head within a silver circle.

Chapter Thirty-One

Zara had just started speaking. 'It's our uncle. He's been . . .'

'Been wandering round the Arctic,' Sam interrupted, loudly. 'Our Uncle Jack,' he blustered on, saying the first name that came to mind. 'He had this mad idea of walking to Nordbergen. Even though everyone knows it's totally uninhabited.'

Fortunately, Officer Ormstad was looking too closely at Sam to notice Ben and Zara's expressions of horrified astonishment. Zara almost butted back in but something made her and Ben hold their tongues. After everything they'd been through, they trusted Sam, even if he seemed to have lost his mind.

'A friend brought us here to ask if anyone had seen him,' Sam pressed on, hoping his face wasn't going as red as it felt. 'But to be honest, we reckon he's given up and headed for home. Isn't that right?' Sam turned to the others. Would they back him up?

'Oh . . . er . . . yeah,' stammered Zara. Sam had better have a good reason for this. 'He's . . . er . . . always saying he's gonna do things, then never doing them, is our Uncle Jack.'

'Probably never even got this far,' added Ben.

'But you said it was urgent,' said Officer Ormstad, frowning. 'Why don't you tell me a few more details? Maybe I can help you anyway.'

'No, it's all right,' said Sam, standing up. 'We got a bit carried away, that's all. Sorry for wasting your time.' He walked to the door and Ben and Zara followed.

Officer Ormstad stood up and, for a moment, Sam was

sure he was going to stop them leaving. Then he seemed to think better of it. 'Well, don't go off anywhere without letting me know,' he said, still frowning.

The children left the building in silence. As soon as they were outside, Zara hissed, 'Have you gone mad, Sam? I know he was a bit stern but he was going to help us. What was wrong?'

'Wait!' whispered Sam. 'Let's get back into Bjørn's Bar.'

They paused in the small vestibule between the outer and inner doors to the bar.

'He's working for Professor Murdo,' said Sam. 'I saw a jacket in his locker with that raven's head emblem on the shoulder. Just like Major Smedling's.'

'Are you sure?' said Ben.

'I'm absolutely sure,' said Sam. 'And thanks for backing me up.'

'It was when I mentioned Nordbergen that he was so keen to get us on his own,' Zara said as the realization struck her. 'I nearly told him everything! I told him too much anyway.'

'I don't think you did,' Sam said. 'He's got nothing to connect us with your uncle and the others.'

'Maybe not,' said Ben. 'But how are we going to rescue them now?'

No one said anything. The full hopelessness of the situation sank in. Olaf had disappeared. His replacement was working for Murdo. They were no better off than they had been at Frank and Yuri's and they had lost another day for nothing.

'We'd better talk to Bjørn,' said Sam. 'He seems a good bloke.'

Ben and Zara nodded and they went in. Bjørn was their only hope. But it didn't seem very likely that he could summon special rescue forces in the next twelve hours.

The customers had returned to their tables. There was no sign of Bjørn but a boy of about seventeen gave them a wave from behind the bar. 'Take a seat by the fire,' he said, 'and I'll bring you some more soup. Bjørn's with Yuri.'

Zara realized guiltily that she had temporarily forgotten about Yuri. 'How is he?' she asked as the boy came over with a tray.

'He started mumbling a little but he's sleeping again now,' said the boy. 'They think he'll be all right though. Severe concussion but no lasting damage. So don't look so down. You saved his life!'

Ben shrugged modestly. 'We were saving our own lives too,' he said.

The boy sat down beside them as they ate their soup. He had a stocky build with broad shoulders and an open, golden-brown face. 'How did you get on with Officer Ormstad?' he asked. 'Tell me to mind my own business, but I wouldn't trust him. *His* mobile phone is working, for a start. I've seen him using it, through his office window.'

'Oh, no!' said Zara. He'd be phoning Nordbergen now. She was sure of it.

The boy's almond-shaped eyes took in the children's strained expressions.

'You're really desperate about something, aren't you?' he said. 'And it's not just Yuri . . . something about your uncle, I heard you say earlier. And something about Nordbergen.'

The children said nothing.

'I'm sorry,' said the boy. 'I'm not trying to be nosy. But I was curious. My mother and father were Nordbergers, you see. Among the last to leave, thirty years ago.'

'Really?' said Zara.

'Yep. My mother's dead now but my father never stops going on about the tragedy of Nordbergen. He never got over leaving. Says he used to be an important man there when he was young. But I don't really know the whole story. I've never known him sober enough to tell it properly.' For a second, the boy's face clouded over with pain. Then he shook his head and smiled ruefully. 'I'm sorry. I came over to see if I could help you, not depress you with my family history.' He extended his right hand. 'My name's Netchek, by the way. Netchek Pietronaq.'

'I'm Zara,' said Zara as they each shook his hand. 'And this is Ben and Sam.'

'Pietronaq?' exclaimed Ben. 'Is your father Thor Pietronaq?'

'Yes,' said Netchek. 'But how did you know that?'

'Our uncle knew your father when he was leader of the Nordbergen government,' said Ben. 'And now our uncle's been kidnapped and taken back there. By the same man who ruined it all the first time.'

'He's going to be killed tomorrow unless we can rescue him!' despaired Zara. 'Olaf was our last chance.'

'Wait!' said Netchek. He turned his head, listening to the sound of a snowmobile approaching and rattling to a halt outside. 'That'll be my girlfriend, Nika, coming in for her evening shift behind the bar. We'll both help you.'

The doors opened and a tall blonde girl in a leather peaked cap walked in. She was about the same age as Netchek and strikingly beautiful. She had no right arm and wore the right sleeve of her leather coat pinned up across her chest, like pictures Ben had seen of Lord Nelson. She greeted Netchek with a kiss and shook hands with the children as Netchek introduced them. 'Nika, this is Zara, Ben and Sam. They urgently need our help.'

Nika sat down. 'Then please tell me everything,' she said, in a Russian accent almost as strong as Yuri's.

The boys turned to Zara. Zara paused. How could these two teenage bar-workers help them? But there was no one else. Quickly but thoroughly she told their whole story, missing out only the method by which they had travelled to Barents Terminus.

'I saw your ice yacht in the harbour just now,' said Nika, when Zara had finished. 'That's some job you did on old Yuri's ski-boat. But one thing I do not understand. You say your uncle was kidnapped on Sunday night. How did you get from Edinburgh to Frank and Yuri's place so quick? Did you get a plane to Murmansk? By yourselves? Have you so much money?'

Zara thought for a moment. 'I'd tell you if I could,' she said. 'But the way we travelled is secret and it's not our secret to tell. Professor Gauntraker left instructions for us when he was kidnapped. It's his secret really.'

Nika said nothing. She studied the children in turn, looking into their eyes. If she *really* wants to know about the ISNT, I'll have to tell her, thought Zara. If she can really help rescue Uncle Alexander, I'll tell her anything.

At last Nika spoke. 'I like you,' she said to all three of them. 'I like your loyalty, I like your courage and I like your ability to keep a secret. I will take you to Nordbergen tonight and we will rescue your uncle and his friends.'

She sounded so confident.

'That's . . . that's so kind of you,' stuttered Zara. 'But how can you . . .'

'Are you ready to leave now?' asked Nika.

'Er . . . yeah,' said Ben. 'We've just got to get our bags from the ski-boat.'

'You three do that,' ordered Nika. 'Netchek, you explain to Bjørn that he must manage without his bar staff for tonight. And tell him to keep Officer Ormstad away from

Yuri. I have one little job to do. Meet out the front, by the snowmobiles, in three minutes.'

By the time the children came back up the harbour steps with their rucksacks, Nika and Netchek were waiting by their snowmobiles. Ben and Zara squeezed onto the back of Nika's, Sam sat behind Netchek, the engines fired and they were off.

They sped past the police station just as Officer Ormstad emerged. Sam looked back to see him leap onto a sleek black snowmobile. Nika and Netchek turned right. They were several hundred metres along a narrow, snow–covered road, heading inland, before Ormstad's headlight came into view.

They sped out of the village and up a steep hill. Sam looked back. Ormstad was catching up. Only fifty metres away . . . twenty metres . . . ten . . . Headlight dazzling Sam's eyes . . . Alongside them, swerving, trying to force Netchek's machine off the road.

But suddenly, the black snowmobile dropped back, engine spluttering to a standstill. Sam caught a brief glimpse of Ormstad's angry face receding into the darkness. Then the stationary headlight disappeared from view as the road twisted up into the hills.

After driving for a further twenty minutes, through a towering landscape of snow and black rock, Nika turned off onto an even narrower track, which meandered down to a desolate cove at the edge of the frozen sea. Nika pulled up next to the only building, a windowless concrete bunker close to the shore. She and Netchek switched off their engines and there was absolute silence.

'It was lucky that Ormstad's snowmobile broke down just when it did,' remarked Netchek, as he climbed stiffly from his seat.

'It was lucky that Bjørn keeps plenty of sugar in his kitchen,' said Nika unlocking the bunker's metal door. 'I put two kilos into Ormstad's petrol tank before we set off, in case he tried to follow us. Don't worry,' she added. 'I left Bjørn some money for it. I'm a saboteur but not a thief.'

Nika slid back the door and went in, turning on a light switch inside.

'Come on,' said Netchek and, mystified, the children followed him into the bunker.

They found themselves in a dimly lit space that smelt of oil and seawater. A rectangle of dark slushy water took up most of the floor space. Nika took what looked like a TV remote control from her pocket and pressed a button. A curved black object rose up through the surface, almost filling the six-metre pool. The object's whale-shaped body had a window at the front, portholes in the side and several angular fins at the rear.

'A submarine!' exclaimed Sam.

'Nika's submarine,' said Netchek, proudly.

'That is how we will get to Nordbergen,' announced Nika. 'We will go under the ice.'

Chapter Thirty-Two

'The Ledrafovich S-67 Five-Man Spy Sub,' said Nika as she pulled the vessel to the edge of the pool by its mooring rope. 'One of twenty built for the Russian navy. Equipped with silent-running electric engines, GPS navigation and sonar. Also an anti-sonar device for avoiding detection.' She climbed up four rungs built into the hull, and opened a metal hatch on top of the submarine. 'Air supplies for five people for forty-eight hours. All aboard.' She disappeared down the hatch.

'On you go,' said Netchek to the children. 'I'll get the snowmobiles into the bunker and lock up.'

A submarine! In spite of his tiredness, Sam was first up to the hatchway. A metal ladder led down to the driving cabin. Five seats faced the wide, curved window and a bank of dials, lights and switches.

Nika was already seated at the steering wheel, her face illuminated by the soft green glow of the control panels. As the children took their seats, Netchek joined them in the cabin. 'Hatch down; airlock secure,' he said.

'OK,' replied Nika, sliding a lever.

The submarine began to descend. Dark water washed up over the window, a gurgling stream of silver bubbles ascending on each side, until they were completely submerged.

By the headlamp's powerful beam, the children could see that they were facing an underwater tunnel.

'This is a purpose-built submarine shed,' explained Nika, driving her vessel into the tunnel. 'Relic of the Cold War.'

'We had to make a few repairs,' said Netchek. 'Like fixing the tide-turbine heater which keeps the sea water in here just above freezing.'

'But where did you get this submarine from?' asked Zara.

'I won it from a gangster in Murmansk, in a game of canasta,' said Nika. 'Where *he* got it from, I did not like to ask. But for this reason, and many other reasons, I decided to leave Russia. I never meant to stay long in Petrøya but I met Netchek.'

'As soon as we've saved up a bit of money working at Bjørn's Bar, we're off,' said Netchek. 'We're going to work our way around the world.'

The submarine passed out of the tunnel. 'The open sea,' announced Nika.

The children leaned forward and looked up. They could just make out the turquoise underside of the pack ice, several metres above them, until it faded into obscurity as Nika took the submarine deeper. She drove the submarine as confidently as she had driven her snowmobile. Occasionally she held the steering wheel steady with her knee whilst reaching out her one hand to operate one of the many controls. Netchek sat next to her, taking charge of the sonar and navigation instruments.

They passed almost silently through the ocean. The water was clear but very dark. Their lights picked up tiny shrimp-like krill and, from time to time, they could see fish, darting away. Once, they passed through a shoal of jelly-fish; beautiful, unearthly creatures whose transparent forms glowed in the headlamp beam.

'You three should get some sleep,' said Netchek after a while. 'We won't reach Nordbergen till dawn.'

'Beds aft,' said Nika, pointing to the doorway behind them.

It had been a long day. Zara, Ben and Sam gratefully stumbled through to the rear cabin, pulled off their boots and snowsuits and flopped into three of the wall-mounted bunk beds. They were too tired to talk now, too tired to look out of the portholes, too tired to lie awake worrying about the problems of the day to come. As the submarine slid silently on through the inky depths, the children sank into sleep.

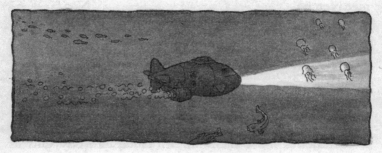

'Ladies and gentlemen. This is your captain speaking. We arrive at Nordbergen in half an hour. Please make your way to the front cabin, where breakfast is now being served.'

Nika's voice, coming through a loudspeaker above the bunks, roused the children from their dreams. Ben looked out of the porthole window beside his head. Was the bluey-green water a little less dark than it had been? He checked his watch. 5.45 a.m.

The three children quickly washed, toileted, put their boots on and went through to the driving cabin, where Netchek handed them each a few cereal bars and a can of orange juice. 'Sorry it's not much of a breakfast,' he apologized. 'Didn't have time to stock up.'

'It's fine,' said Zara. She felt too nervous to eat much anyway. This was it. Their last day to rescue Uncle Alexander.

'What's the plan when we get to Nordbergen?' asked Ben, voicing the question they were all thinking.

'First we must arrive without being detected,' said Nika. 'And that may not be easy, even with our anti-sonar device. Our main weapon is that the enemy do not know we are here – and we must not lose that advantage.' She extinguished the headlamp and dimmed the control-panel lights to their lowest level. 'Did Professor Gauntraker tell you anything about the security arrangements on Nordbergen?' she asked.

'An armed garrison, he said,' remembered Sam. 'With planes, snowmobiles and surveillance equipment. It sounded pretty heavy.'

'We must hope they have nothing underwater,' said Nika. 'We will go in slowly.'

The water was definitely paler now, especially above them. Way way up, the children could just make out the underside of the ice again, a faint glimmer of daylight showing through a few translucent blue patches.

Now the rocky seabed came into view and they followed its upward slope until the icy surface lay only fifteen metres or so above them. The underside of the ice looked to Zara like an inverted image of the icescape they had travelled over the day before, with pressure ridges hanging down and ice gullies soaring upwards. Suddenly, looming through the turquoise water ahead,

they could see rocks; steep, tall rocks, some disappearing up through the ice. They had reached the edge of Nordbergen.

'Maybe we can find a break in the ice and use our periscope,' said Nika, edging the submarine slowly round the rocks.

Suddenly, from around a distant outcrop ahead of them, a light appeared; a single white light in the centre of a dark shadowy shape. Another submarine!

Nika instantly threw her sub into a diving turn which nearly flung the children from their seats, and darted for cover.

'Crevice to starboard!' yelled Netchek.

Her hand flashing from lever to steering wheel, Nika span the sub around and reversed into the underwater cave. Their rudder fin clunked the back of the hollow before their nose was fully inside. Were they hidden? Had they been spotted?

'No talking,' breathed Nika, plunging the control panel into total darkness. 'They may have listening devices.'

The other submarine cruised into view, barely twenty metres from their hiding place. Its streamlined grey hull, twice the length of their vessel, bore the raven's head emblem. It turned this way and that, its powerful search-light scanning each rock face and gully. There could be no doubt that they *had* been spotted, and not much doubt that they would be found again at any moment.

The beam probed relentlessly, coming closer and closer. Nika held her hand on the accelerator lever, ready to make a run for it.

Then another object swam into view, gliding across the space between themselves and the other submarine: a massive creature with the creviced skin of an elephant, the tail flippers of a sea lion and the long front fins of a whale. The searchlight

170

flicked onto the animal, illuminating two white tusks hanging down from its mouth.

With effortless speed, the walrus rolled out of the light, swooped under the enemy sub and disappeared into the distant gloom. The submarine span round to watch the walrus go, then sat motionless for a few seconds. The children held their breaths, looking up at the stern of the enemy vessel.

Apparently satisfied that what had been sighted had been the walrus all along, the enemy submarine began to ease away from the rocks. The children expected Nika to wait until it had gone completely but, to their astonishment, she pulled back the accelerator lever and drove out of the cave before the enemy had gone more than a few metres.

Focusing intently on the windowless rear of the other submarine, Nika manoeuvred her own craft silently up beneath its rudder. Sam was sure they were going to collide but Nika slid them forward with unbelievable precision until they were directly beneath the enemy's hull, with barely a metre between the two vessels.

The enemy submarine steered a course around Nord-bergen's undersea coastline and Nika followed its every movement as if she could read its captain's mind. It would only take the tiniest error for them to be seen instantly by the enemy. Remembering Nika's warning, everyone remained silent.

After an anxious twenty minutes, the enemy submarine took them into a wide gully in the rock face. Just before they reached what appeared to be a dead end, the grey vessel swerved into an almost concealed opening on one side. Nika just managed to keep position as they entered a narrow passageway.

It grew darker. Presumably the ice above the enemy submarine had given way to rock. Zara realized now that Nika had been right to chance such a daring strategy: they would never have found this way in to Nordbergen by themselves. It still seemed terribly risky but Zara drove down the fear inside her. If this tunnel took them nearer to where Uncle Alexander was being held, any risk was worth taking.

The underwater passage opened out into a rectangular tank, similar to the one in Nika's submarine shed, but much bigger. The enemy submarine rose to the surface. One or two metallic clanks resounded through the water and the vessel rocked slightly. Sam guessed that the crew were disembarking.

Nika waited until all had been still for several minutes before reversing, then ascending into the space behind the enemy vessel. She stopped before they broke surface however, and pressed a button.

A tiny video camera emerged from a hatch on the sub's nose and rose through the surface on a telescopic rod. They all studied the grainy black-and-white monitor screen as Nika rotated the electronic periscope through 360°. The enemy submarine . . . slit windows high in the concrete side walls . . . stacked-up crates and fuel drums . . . a door in the end wall . . . no people.

Nika nodded, withdrew the camera and completed their ascent. Still in silence, they all donned their outdoor clothing.

'Bring anything which might be useful,' whispered Nika to the children as Netchek put a few tools into his small backpack. 'Netchek, you go out first. Check no one has remained in their sub. And sabotage it, to prevent pursuit later.'

Ben and Zara took their torches from their rucksacks. Sam stuffed his torch, clock-compass and Swiss army knife into various pockets and hung his binoculars round his neck. It didn't seem much with which to take on an armed garrison. Their mouths felt dry.

Through their window, they watched Netchek peer into the enemy submarine's portholes before clambering onto its hull and disappearing down its unlocked hatchway, wire cutters in hand. Two minutes later, he re-emerged, grinning and giving them a thumbs-up.

They all managed the short leap from the submarine to the edge of the pool, which, as they had seen on the periscope monitor, lay in the centre of a concrete shed.

'Let's have a look out,' said Nika, leading them to the door, and peeping through its reinforced glass window.

They gasped with surprise at the sight that met their eyes. Towering a hundred metres above them, its silver body gilded by the rising sun, stood the colossal figure of a man.

Chapter Thirty-Three

'What *is* it?' said Zara, as they stared at the silver colossus.

Had Professor Murdo been working all this time to create a huge robot? No. The figure didn't look as if it had been built to move. It stood with its legs together and its arms outstretched from each side of its smooth, stylized body. The fingers of its open hands were curved slightly forward, as if it were about to embrace the air in front of it. Its domed head faced dead ahead, its eyes seeming to stare into the distance. The searching gaze, together with the aloof line of its mouth, conveyed an impression of cold intelligence.

'Is it a statue?' Nika wondered.

'I think it's a building,' said Ben. 'Look, I reckon that's a big window across its chest. And that's probably a door between its feet.'

'You're right,' agreed Sam, surveying the figure with his binoculars. 'There are other windows too, I think, like the eyes. And there, in one of the arms. I can't see in, though. Must be special mirrored glass.'

'If your uncle and the others are being held in there, it's not going to be easy to reach them,' observed Nika. 'But there are other outbuildings, see? I think this submarine shed is part of a circle of huts going around the giant man.'

'Let's see what's to the side of us,' suggested Netchek. He hoisted himself up onto a stack of wooden crates and peered through a high window in one of the side walls. 'Come and look,' he whispered, giving them a hand up.

They gazed across a square of ice-covered tarmac, into the wide-open doors of an aircraft hangar. Four men were sliding a small aircraft into the hangar, on its skis. The aircraft was grey and angular with the raven motif on its tail. Inside the hangar, two larger aircraft could be seen.

'I reckon it was one of those big planes that Uncle Alexander and the others were kidnapped in,' said Sam.

'That small one looks as if it's just arrived,' said Ben.

'Professor Murdo!' groaned Zara. 'I bet *he* just arrived in it. We've got here too late!'

'Er . . . hello.'

They all span round at the sound of a female voice. A small figure dressed in a black snowsuit emerged from behind another pile of crates by the opposite wall. 'It's all right!' the girl's voice said quickly. 'I . . . I'm not one of the people from this place. You're not either, are you? Are you here to rescue someone? I heard you talking. Please, can you help me?' She looked and sounded as scared as they were, thought Zara.

'Who are you?' snapped Nika, poised for action on top of her crate. 'Are you alone?'

'Y—yes, I'm alone. My name's Marcia. Marcia Slick. I was brought here by my parents. Th—they drugged me. Had me locked up. They were going to have me . . . have me *operated* on. My face . . . my genes . . . Make me a different person . . . But I escaped. Hid.'

'How long have you been hiding here?' asked Nika, less harshly, coming down to floor level, followed by the three children.

'Since yesterday morning. There's heating in here and I found food in one of the crates. I kept expecting them to search in here for me. Maybe they didn't think I could've left the main building. I got *some* sleep till a load of men came in, in the middle of the night. I was really scared. But they went off in their submarine. They just came back, before you arrived. Where *is* this place? I know we're in the Arctic.'

'The island of Nordbergen, in the Barents Sea.'

'You'll take me with you, won't you?' pleaded Marcia. 'I thought I was never going to get away from here. I've been watching the hangar, hoping I might get a chance to stow away on one of the planes. But they haven't gone anywhere. And there are guards. I–I can't stand much more of this. Please help me.'

'You're with us now,' promised Nika, putting her arm around Marcia's shoulders. 'I'm Nika. This is Netchek, Zara, Ben and Sam.'

'Here,' said Netchek, passing down several cereal bars and a bottle of juice from his lookout post by the windows.

'We can't leave until we've rescued six people who are imprisoned here,' said Nika. 'It will be dangerous. Do you want to wait in the submarine? You look shattered.'

'No, I'm all right,' said Marcia, feeling stronger now that she wasn't alone any more. 'I'll help you, if I can.'

'Have you seen four men and two women, being held prisoner?' asked Zara. 'All in their sixties.'

Marcia shook her head. 'I'm sorry. I didn't see any other prisoners.'

'Did you see that small plane arrive?' asked Sam.

'Yes. About twenty minutes ago, before the submarine came back. I saw Dr Marmwell – he's the man who arranged with my parents to bring me here – I saw him come over to meet the pilot. I could hear them talking when they walked back past here. Dr Marmwell called the pilot Professor Murdo. I think he's in charge. He was the one who was going to operate on me. Dr Marmwell was telling him that I'd escaped. He was really grovelling but Professor Murdo said that it didn't matter any more and to have my parents brought up to his lab in half an hour with . . . what did he say? . . . With the six professors.'

'*That's them!*' exclaimed Zara. 'That's the prisoners. Our uncle and five of his friends. Do you know where Murdo's lab is?'

'No,' said Marcia. 'I'm sorry. But it's got to be somewhere in that weird building. I was being kept in one of the arms.'

'We've got to get in!' said Ben. 'And fast. He's gonna kill our uncle and the others.'

'I don't know how we could get in,' said Marcia. 'The main doors are between the feet but there's armed guards and everything. It was nearly impossible to get out.'

'Hmm. It will be difficult without inside information,' said Nika.

'Men approaching!' warned Netchek from the windows. 'They've finished putting that plane away. Two of them have stayed to guard the hangar but the other two are coming this way. Get ready to hide. They might come in here.'

As they all squatted down behind the crates, two voices came into audible range from outside.

'Can't we have a break, Steve? I'm knackered.'

'Shut it, Gary. We've gotta clean all the toilets in the outside huts this morning.'

'Aw, come on!'

'I'll do the ones over at the snowmobile depot. You start here in the sub shed and work your way round.'

''S not fair!'

'It's Gary!' hissed Marcia. 'I think he'd do anything to leave this place.'

There was only time for the briefest whispered discussion before the door of the submarine shed began to creak open.

As Gary entered, Nika and Netchek stepped out from behind the crates. With balaclavas right up over their noses, it was hard to tell they were only seventeen.

'Stay exactly where you are, Gary,' Nika rapped out.

Gary stared at the newcomers. The gun-shaped electric screwdriver that Netchek was pointing at him looked enough like a real weapon for Gary to obey Nika's order. 'Uh? Who are you?' he croaked.

'We are the advance party of a massive international invasion force,' lied Nika. 'I have thousands of assault troops waiting offshore and dozens of aircraft waiting to strike. Nordbergen Research Enterprises is about to become history. All those involved in its criminal activities will find themselves in BIG TROUBLE.'

'I never done anything!' protested Gary. 'I hate it here. They said I was gonna drive a snowmobile and stuff but it's rubbish.'

'You work here,' snapped Nika. 'You're one of the enemy.'

'I'm not! I don't wanna be. I never wanted to work here. I could help *you*.'

'Hmm. Maybe we *could* find use for an inside agent. But it is very difficult work.'

'I could do it! Just tell me what you want me to do.'

'I need to get six of us into the main building. Now. Before the assault. We need to get into Professor Murdo's lab.'

'But *I* can't get you in past the guards!' wailed Gary. 'I wanna help you, honest, but security's really tight, specially since some girl ran away from upstairs. And no one can go up to Murdo's lab without special authorization. 'S right up in the head.'

'Is there no way in other than the main door?'

Gary thought hard. 'There's a few maintenance hatches.

'Only one at ground level, on the back of the right heel. The hatches don't go right into the building; just into the space between the outer and inner walls. There's a ladder in there. I dunno if it goes right up to the head but Steve says he went up to the shoulders once, when they were still building it.'

'Is this hatch guarded?'

'No, but there's an alarm and cameras covering the area,' said Gary. 'But I know where they switch off. There's a big board in the guardroom, in the left foot. Steve knows one of the officers who work there. We go in for a drink sometimes. He'll be on shift now.'

'Then go there,' ordered Nika. 'Find a way to switch off the alarm and cameras when the guard is not looking. Can you do that?'

'I'll do it,' said Gary. 'I'll find a way. As long as I can go home.'

'We'll see that you get home,' promised Nika.

'Give me five minutes,' said Gary, leaving the shed. 'You'll need time to get round the back of the building. There's never anyone round that side. When the red light on the camera goes out, you'll know I've switched it off. But I won't be able to keep it off for long.'

Marcia, Zara, Ben and Sam waited until Gary was well away from the shed before they emerged from the crates.

'Let's go,' said Nika.

Quickly but cautiously, they stumbled over the icy ground behind the ring of outbuildings, fuelling up on cereal bars as they went. They checked there was no one on the path before dashing across the exposed spaces between one building and the next. It was as they were crossing such a gap, halfway round to the back of the giant man, that Nika slipped over on the ice.

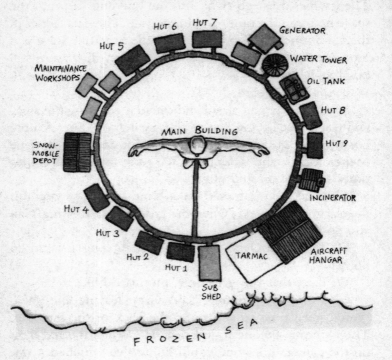

'Keep going,' Netchek ordered the children, pausing to help Nika. The children reached the cover of the next Portakabin and looked back to see Netchek pulling Nika back to her feet.

'FREEZE!' A man's voice rang out from the path at the front of the outbuildings. 'Stay where you are, both of you, or I'll shoot!'

Chapter Thirty-Four

Ben felt Zara tug his arm and pull him into the space beneath the raised Portakabin. Sam and Marcia followed. Ben could see the black snow boots of the security guard striding towards Nika and Netchek.

'Who are you? What are you doing here?' he barked.

'My name's Marcia Slick,' came Nika's voice. 'I escaped from in there.' Quick thinking, thought Ben.

'I—I'm— Joe,' stammered Netchek. 'I work here. She persuaded me to help her.'

'Department?' snapped the guard.

'Er . . . cleaning.'

'Anyone else with you?'

'No,' said Netchek.

Ben watched the guard's feet stomp towards the back of the Portakabin. Had they left footprints? No, thank goodness; the surface was frozen solid. Apparently satisfied, the guard moved back to Nika and Netchek, talking into his radio.

'Sergeant Lynch to Major Smedling. Sergeant Lynch to Major Smedling. Over.'

'Major Smedling to Sergeant Lynch,' came the crackling reply. 'Make your report. Over.'

'Have apprehended Marcia Slick. Also one of our cleaners. Both trying to escape. Over.'

'Good work, Sergeant. Where are you? Over.'

'Beside Hut Eight. Over.'

'Put them in Hut Three. Guard them and await further instructions. I'm fully occupied over here with Professor

Murdo. Speak shortly. Over and out.'

The guard marched Nika and Netchek away.

'Come on,' hissed Zara, rolling out from under the Porta-kabin. 'We've got to get to that hatch.'

Marcia hesitated. 'But it might have been Gary who sent the guard.'

'I don't think so,' said Zara. 'Or the guard wouldn't have believed Nika. And he'd have known there were six of us.'

The four children reached the huts directly behind the figure without further incident.

'We'll rescue Nika and Netchek after,' whispered Zara. 'But we've got to help Uncle Alexander and the others first, before it's too late.'

'There's the hatch,' said Sam, using his binoculars. 'I can see two cameras.'

'Are the red lights on?' asked Marcia.

'Yes, they're— no, they've just gone off!'

'There's no one about,' hissed Ben, checking the path in both directions. 'Come on!'

They left the cover of the hut, crossed the path and raced across the icy ground. A short metal ladder led up to the hatch. The steel panel, less than a metre square, was hinged down one edge and held shut by a line of screws down the other.

'Netchek's got all the tools,' Ben said in dismay.

'We've still got my Swiss army knife,' said Sam, wrestling with the first of the screws.

As soon as Sam had loosened each screw, he hurried onto the next, leaving the others to twist the screws out with their fingers; an awkward task with thick gloves on. Zara glanced up at the dormant eye of the camera above them. How long did they have?

At last the final screw came out. They swung the hatch open, scrambled through and pulled it shut behind them. It was pitch dark.

They heard a dull click, followed by a continuous electrical hum. 'I reckon that's the alarm and cameras back on,' said Ben. 'We were only just in time.' He switched on his torch, illuminating a metal ladder that disappeared up through the complex inner construction of the legs. Zara switched on her torch, jammed it into her top pocket, so it shone upwards, and started to climb. The cold had drained them of energy but there was no time to lose. 'Try not to clank,' she advised the others, 'or someone'll hear us inside.'

'What's the plan if we get to the head?' whispered Marcia, following Ben and Sam.

'Let's get there first,' puffed Zara, avoiding the question to which none of them had an answer.

They climbed without pause for twenty minutes. Sometimes the ladder took them straight up. Sometimes it twisted round the overhanging contours of the figure. Occasionally they passed other hatchways and platforms leading to complicated arrangements of pipes or cables. They ignored these and pressed on upwards. Above them, endless metalwork loomed into the range of their torches. Below them, the steps they had climbed faded into a black void.

At last, the top of the ladder came into view. It ended beside a round hatch set into the outer wall. Zara slid back a bolt, pushed it open and put her head out.

Bright blue sky. Freezing wind. Metal railings. They had emerged through the nape of the figure's neck, onto a railed metal walkway that stretched away to either side, over the figure's shoulders.

Legs aching, they clambered out onto the narrow strip of steel. It felt terrifyingly high; high enough to see the whole island of Nordbergen spread out beneath them. The metal railings vibrated with a high-pitched hum in the wind.

They moved gingerly along the icy walkway, first one way, then the other, looking up at their destination; the figure's head. Metal rungs protruded from both sides of the neck, leading up to each enormous ear. Both ears, they could now see, had satellite dishes and aerials built in to them and it was presumably for the maintenance of these that the steps existed.

'Let's not hang about,' said Ben starting to climb the rungs to the left ear. 'If we can't get in this ear, we'll try the other one.'

Although none of them was normally scared of heights, they each found the exposed climb up the side of the neck and face the most frightening thing they had ever had to do. Sam tried to tell himself it was no different from climbing a ladder at ground level. Then he glanced down and felt his legs trembling. Somehow he forced himself on, looking only upwards.

They all made it to the top and helped each other onto the small platform set just inside the ear. Zara put her finger to her lips and pointed to a hinged panel at the back of the ear cavity. It was similar to the hatch in the heel except that it had a door handle and no screws holding it shut. There appeared to be no surveillance cameras up here and Zara hoped there were also no door alarms as she opened the hatch ajar and peered inside.

The hatchway led into a cramped space, filled with more

satellite and radio equipment. At the back of the space was another door. They crept towards it. Voices could be heard from the other side. Harsh, indignant voices.

'I am an international media celebrity. I demand to be released!'

'You'll pay for this, Marmwell! You'll pay for this, big time!'

'It's my parents,' whispered Marcia.

The voices didn't sound very close to the door and Zara risked opening it by just a few millimetres. The door led onto a curved mezzanine which ran around the back wall of the vast space. There was nobody on it. A meshed screen of black metal ran along the front edge and Zara could see beyond this to two huge eye-shaped windows. But she couldn't see down into the main part of the room, from where the voices were coming. Crouching, she opened the door just enough to squeeze through and led the others onto the mezzanine. They crawled forward and looked down through the meshing.

The room took up the lower half of the head. The flat ceiling, just above the eye windows, was three metres above the mezzanine; the shiny black floor was five metres below them. A transparent pillar descended from the centre of the ceiling to the middle of the floor. In front of this stood a massive console of computers, switches and buttons.

Eight metal chairs were arranged in a semicircle, like teeth in the giant figure's jaw, facing the console. Marcus and Alicia Slick sat in the two furthest chairs, clamped firmly by steel bands around their ankles and wrists. Dr Marmwell and Major Smedling, ignoring the Slicks' protests, were ordering twelve armed guards to fasten six people into the remaining chairs: Professor Gauntraker, Professor Sharpe, Professor Pottle, Professor Hartleigh-

Broadbeam, Professor Gadling and Professor Ampersand.

Zara and Ben's hearts leapt. The professors looked terribly bedraggled. Their uncle looked thin, exhausted and unshaven. But he was alive. Their uncle was still alive.

The children watched as the professors were thrust into the chairs, the wrist and ankle bands clicking into place as a single lever was pulled down on each chair's back. Sam's mind raced, unable to think of a way of overcoming so many armed men.

'Professor Murdo will be here for his little chat soon,' sneered Major Smedling. 'Then I'll be taking you for your underwater swim with the penguins.'

'There aren't any penguins in the Arctic,' came six weary voices, almost in unison.

'*I knew that!*' screamed Smedling. '*Bleeding scientists!*'

'Are the prisoners all secure, Major?' asked Dr Marmwell.

'Yes, Doctor,' grunted Smedling.

'Then dismiss your men,' instructed Dr Marmwell. 'Professor Murdo wishes this to be a private session.'

'All right, men,' ordered Smedling. 'Back in the lift and wait downstairs. I'll call you up if you're needed.'

The twelve guards trooped away beneath the mezzanine, from where the whirr of lift doors could be heard. The children looked at each other. Only one armed man in the room. But Major Smedling was standing on the far side, covering the whole space with his gun.

Dr Marmwell spoke into an intercom on the console: 'All ready, Professor Murdo.' He and Smedling looked up expectantly at the top of the transparent pillar. After a few seconds, a tall figure in a white lab coat descended into view, standing on a disc that transported him down the centre of the pillar. The disc landed with a hiss, the

doors of the pneumatic elevator slid open and Professor
Roderick Murdo strode into the room.

Chapter Thirty-Five

'Together again,' declared Professor Murdo in a clear resounding voice. 'The Seven Professors of the Far North.'

In contrast to his erstwhile colleagues' dishevelled state, Professor Murdo was immaculately attired in a crisp white lab coat, worn over a white, high-necked suit. His tanned, handsome face carried an air of arrogance. His mane of hair, swept back from his high forehead, was jet black, except for a streak of white around each temple.

'Are you Professor Murdo?' rapped out Marcus Slick. 'I demand that you release us at once. I demand to know the meaning of this outrageous—'

'You are in no position to demand anything!' snapped Professor Murdo. 'But, believe me, the meaning of all this is about to be made perfectly clear.' He turned to the professors. 'Though I take it that our intrepid friend Eric has already told you all he discovered about my work.'

'He didn't have time to tell us anything before your ruffians abducted us,' said Professor Hartleigh-Broadbeam. 'And we've been held in separate cells since we arrived here.'

'They don't know anything,' growled Professor Gauntraker. 'You might as well let them go.'

'That's very touching, Eric,' said Professor Murdo, 'but I *want* you all to know everything. To recognize my greatness. To see how wrong you were.'

'Greatness?' snorted Alicia Slick. 'Your organization has totally failed to honour its contract with us.'

'Oh, *please!* You're not still under the illusion that the

purpose of this entire research centre is to tinker with the genes of your precious teenage daughter? You people are so vain! Do you really imagine I'd squander my genius on such banal child's play? Clients like you are brought here for two reasons only. Firstly, for the money you bring. It costs a fortune to build and run a place like this. And secondly, to provide me with live research material. Well, live when you arrive. My work has required a constant supply of human donors.'

'You won't get away with this!' screamed Alicia. 'We're not some down-and-outs you can kidnap without anyone noticing!'

'All my donors have been wealthy and privileged,' Professor Murdo told her, calmly. 'You people are so easy to spirit away. You're flattered when Dr Marmwell worms his way into your affections, casually, at some party. He appeals to your vanity. You're *special* people, he tells you. People who deserve the very best for your child. You people are *never* happy with your offspring, so you eagerly lap up what he tells you about our Genetic Modification Treatment. It sounds so *exclusive*. So *unaffordable* to the great unwashed. And you're as keen as he is to keep it all *secret*. You don't even tell your closest friends that you're coming here because you *have* no close friends. The very privileges of your wealth – total privacy, total independence from others – are what makes it so easy to dispose of you secretly.'

'You're mad!' screamed Alicia.

Professor Murdo's eyes blazed. 'These six wretches beside you once thought me mad,' he hissed. 'It's time to show you all how wrong you are. It's time to prove to you all that I am the greatest genius the world has ever known.' He pressed a button on the console, sending the empty pneumatic lift back up through the ceiling. After a few seconds it began to return. Everyone in the room looked up to see a young boy descending.

The boy stepped out of the lift. He appeared to be about seven years old, though his pale, solemn face looked somehow older. His black hair had been cut short and he wore a blue tunic, blue trousers and black boots.

'I'd like you to meet Adam,' said Professor Murdo. 'Adam, show these people some of your skills. Perhaps a back flip to start with, if you please.'–Without any change in his serious expression, the boy sprang up in a standing jump, flipped himself over in mid air and landed back down with both feet on the same spot.

'A one-hand balance,' ordered Professor Murdo.

Adam kicked both legs into the air as his left hand came down to the floor. He remained balanced on the hand for several seconds, without even wobbling.

'Adam, catch!' said Professor Murdo, flinging a handful of loose coins at the boy. Adam thrust himself back to an upright position, his hands flying from coin to coin in a frenzied blur. There must have been nine separate coins, yet not one dropped to the floor.

Professor Murdo took a calculator from his pocket and punched in many numbers at random. 'Four hundred and twenty-eight thousand, three hundred and sixty-nine multiplied by seventy-seven?' he called out.

'Thirty-two million, nine hundred and eighty-four thousand, four hundred and thirteen,' answered Adam instantly.

'Correct.' Professor Murdo held the calculator up to his captive audience. 'Do please call out another sum, to assure yourselves that I hadn't prepared Adam in advance. Or give Adam any sequence of words or numbers to memorize on one hearing. Or . . .'

'I think we get the idea,' interrupted Professor Sharpe. 'We have no wish to put this obviously gifted child through any more demeaning party tricks. Presumably you're about to tell us that he is your son.'

'He is not merely my son,' proclaimed Professor Murdo. 'He is my *creation*. He was conceived by implanting the nucleus from one of my cells into an empty female egg cell taken from a deceased research subject. He was gestated in a so-called artificial womb, designed and built by myself. Yet he is no mere clone. There are hundreds of scientists in the world capable of cloning a human being. I did what no one else had the knowledge to do. Whilst Adam was still in his earliest embryonic stage, I entirely reprogrammed his genetic make-up. Using the knowledge acquired from my decades of research, I modified certain genes, I removed undesirable genes and I added extra genes. I created a new DNA.

'You called Adam a gifted child but you have no idea what gifts I have bequeathed him. The child you see now has developed to only a *fraction* of his ultimate potential. Adam has the appearance of a seven-year-old, the physical co-ordination of an athlete in his prime, the mental abilities of a genius. *Yet I swear to you that Adam is not yet one year old.*'

'*What!*' cried Professor Gadling. 'That can't be true. No human child could grow so fast!'

'*Precisely!*' crowed Professor Murdo. 'Adam *is* no human child. He shares less DNA with modern humans than modern humans do with chimpanzees. *In Adam, I have created the first member of a new species of man. A perfect species. A species which shall inherit the earth.*'

Chapter Thirty-Six

The children stared down through the meshed screen. Could they really be looking at a child who was not human?

'Preposterous!' cried Professor Sharpe. 'One poor genetically modified child does not constitute a new species.'

'But Adam is just the first,' said Professor Murdo. 'Our huge laboratories are ready to go into production. Over the next few months, hundreds of new beings will be created. Like Adam, they'll be freed from the most wasteful stages of a human life: childhood and old age. Members of Adam's species will reach full maturity in just three years, then cease to age at all during their extended life span.'

'And these superhumans are to be developed from cloned embryos of *yourself*, presumably?' sneered Professor Sharpe.

'The clones will be developed from all of us involved in the Nordbergen Project,' chipped in Dr Marmwell. 'We are the Fathers of the Future.'

'The fat-heads of the century, more like,' snorted Professor Hartleigh-Broadbeam.

'You're just bitter because *your* genes won't be carried into the New Era,' sneered Major Smedling.

'You think Murdo's going to let *you* in on this?' shouted Professor Gadling. 'Can't you see he's planning to clone this supposedly perfect race entirely from himself? He's barking mad!'

'There's nothing mad about seeking perfection!' railed Professor Murdo. 'Everybody wants people to be perfect.

How many foetuses are aborted each year simply because tests show they would have been born imperfect? How many women have been sterilized by their governments before they could even *conceive* children who might have been imperfect?'

'We don't all approve of eugenics,' said Professor Ampersand.

'We all know deep down that human development is ultimately a quest for perfection,' Professor Murdo continued. 'Why else do we make school children sit so many tests? Why else do people worry that they're too fat, too thin, too tall, too short, too this or too that? We're all drawn to perfection as inexorably as a plant is drawn to the sunlight. All I've done is to admit it. All I've done is taken logical steps to achieve it. Humanity as we know it is inherently flawed. It will never be perfected. I have had to create a new species.'

'Well, bully for you,' said Professor Hartleigh–Broadbeam flatly. 'But you might find your own species has something to say about your murderous research methods.'

'Today's humanity will never accept my creation's rightful place in the destiny of mankind, just as it has never accepted my genius. My father scorned me, my teachers derided me, you six betrayed me. I will not allow Adam and his descendants to be persecuted the way *I* have been. My new species must be free to build their own laboratories, to create future generations, to populate the planet and the universe beyond. In order for the new species to live, the old humanity must be totally eradicated.'

'Now I *know* you're mad!' shrieked Alicia Slick. 'Eradicate everyone on earth! They'll find out what you're up to and destroy you first, and that freak beside you.'

'A Norwegian police officer called Nansen nearly found out what I'm up to but his body now lies deep beneath the ice,' said Professor Murdo calmly. 'Professor Gauntraker found out what I'm up to and here he is, powerless before me. I admit it's taken a lot of effort to prevent rumours leaking out of the region – jamming telecommunications systems, infiltrating police forces, disposing of the occasional nosy trapper – but now the need for secrecy is over. The Great Purge is about to begin.'

Professor Murdo stepped nearer to his prisoners. 'I have no further need for human research material,' he said. 'I *was* going to send you to the bottom of the sea, to join Officer Nansen. However, I have decided that you should play a more important part in the dawning of the New Era.' From an inside pocket he brought out a tiny canister, no bigger than a jar of ink and made of frosted grey metal. 'This canister contains  *another* new species,' he said softly. 'The first million or so specimens of a new virus. I have just brought it back from a specialist laboratory in Switzerland, where I supervised its creation. This virus is more deadly and more virulent than anything previously known to man. It transmits easily through air. It multiplies at a staggering rate. The chance of infection following exposure is one hundred per cent. Severe symptoms occur within ten minutes. Unconsciousness follows in two hours. Death within twenty-four.'

Sam looked at the others. They *had* to do something soon. But what? Major Smedling still stood beside Dr Marmwell on the far side of the room, covering the space with his gun.

Adam stood impassively in the centre of the console, his wide eyes showing no emotion as Professor Murdo continued. 'The virus has been designed to attack one species and one species only. Humans. It will not affect Adam's species. I have administered a sophisticated genetic inoculation to myself and all my staff. It would take the world's experts years to develop a similar vaccine. If they had years.'

'Roderick, come to your senses!' implored Professor Ampersand. 'We were once friends. You were a brilliant scientist. Everybody knew it. You must turn your back on this destructive work. You mustn't release that virus into the world.'

'Oh, but I'm not going to release it into the world,' smiled Professor Murdo. '*You* are.' He walked over to Professor Ampersand. Major Smedling stepped nearer, his piggy eyes eager for a closer look at the canister of death. Nearer to Professor Murdo; nearer to the children.

'I'm going to open the canister,' stated Professor Murdo. 'Within minutes, the eight of you will be infected. In a few hours, your semiconscious bodies will be parachuted from my stealth planes into eight of the most populous cities in the world. Within weeks, the virus will have taken its grip on the entire planet. Within a year, when Adam and his brethren go forth to claim the Earth, the human race will be all but extinct.'

Professor Murdo raised his fingers above the canister lid. As one, Sam, Zara, Ben and Marcia sprang to their feet and onto the meshed screen. This was it. There was no time to think. No time for clever plans. One desperate chance.

'You two get Smedling!' hissed Zara as she and Ben dived headlong towards Murdo. Sam flung himself at Smedling's neck. Smedling had already spun round; aimed his gun at the mezzanine. *PKKKKKZZZZSSTT!* Sam felt the jet of white fire streaming past him. Saw Ben and Zara cannoning into Murdo. CRACK! He crashed into Smedling's chin. Down on the floor. Marcia with him, clinging to Smedling's arms. *PKKZZSST! PKKZZST!* Smedling's gun firing wildly. Hold onto him! Can't get the gun off him! . . . *ugh!* Someone's hands round neck . . . Marmwell . . . strangling . . . can't breathe . . .

Sam felt himself being pulled back by the throat and flung through the air. He caught a glimpse of Professor Ampersand's astonished face before he slammed into the metal chair.

'*Sam!*' cried Professor Ampersand. 'The lever! On the back!' Ignoring the pain in his cheekbone and his leg, Sam groped for the lever.

Now Marmwell had dragged Marcia off Smedling too. Smedling was back on his feet, trying to kick Ben and Zara clear of Murdo before shooting.

There – the lever! As his metal bonds clicked open, Professor Ampersand launched himself from the chair in a flying tackle. Ben was on his back, mouth bleeding, Smedling aiming at his head and . . . WHAM! *PKKKZZZSST!* Ampersand slammed Smedling over, the weapon firing a blazing torrent across the ceiling.

Sam staggered around the backs of the next five chairs, releasing the other professors. He followed them back into the fray as they sprang from their chairs.

Chaos. Blasts of gunfire. Smedling and Murdo shouting for the guards. Murdo on his feet, punching Zara clear. Pottle, Sharpe and Ben diving onto him. Hartleigh-Broadbeam and Marcia wrestling Marmwell into an empty chair. Marcus and Alicia screaming to be released.

Sam charged to help Ampersand, Gauntraker and Gadling who were grappling with Smedling. *PKKKZZZSST!* Another wild blast blazed over Sam's head, up to the mezzanine and through the wooden door they'd entered by. The door and the inner ear behind it burst into flames.

Chapter Thirty-Seven

Nika and Netchek stood with their backs to the concrete wall inside Hut Three. Sergeant Lynch stood by the door, covering them with his gun. No one had spoken in the forty-five minutes since their capture.

The silence was broken by the sound of footsteps on the track outside. Someone rapped on the steel door. 'Sergeant Lynch, sir. Orders from Major Smedling. You're to bring the prisoners to the main building.'

Without taking his gun off Nika and Netchek, Sergeant Lynch reached behind him, unlocked the door and pushed it open. He took a brief glance at the person outside. It was Gary.

'Come on,' grunted Lynch, keeping his eyes on his prisoners as he backed out through the door. Gary stuck a foot out behind the sergeant's heels and grabbed his right elbow, tugging his fingers from the gun trigger and jerking him violently backwards. Sergeant Lynch swore as he went over onto his back. He fumbled for his gun but a flying kick from Netchek sent it spinning from his grasp.

Netchek knelt on the sergeant's chest and Gary held the gun to his head whilst Nika pulled the radio, revolver and keys from his belt. Within seconds he had been thrust inside the hut.

'Good work, Gary,' said Nika, locking the door.

''S all right,' said Gary modestly. 'I saw you being taken in here when I'd finished in the guardroom.'

'Did you manage to switch off the cameras and alarm?' asked Netchek.

'Yeah. For a few minutes.'

Nika and Netchek looked up at the head of the giant figure. 'Do you think the others –' began Nika but she was interrupted by a violent explosion erupting from the figure's left ear.

'Come on! This way!' she ordered, breaking into a run.

A flailing kick from Smedling sent Sam to the floor. *PKKZZST! PKKZZST!* The gun blasted upwards again, shattering one of the eye windows, as Professors Ampersand, Gauntraker and Gadling tried to pull Smedling's weapon from him. Sam looked round the room. Through a haze of gun smoke, Sam could see Dr Marmwell being clamped into a chair. He could see Professor Murdo being dragged to another. But where was the deadly canister?

There! The small figure of Adam stood in the centre of the room, behind the console. He held the canister in his left hand, whilst his right flitted over the console keyboard with the speed of a concert pianist.

A voice came over the intercom. 'Major Smedling? Professor Murdo? Are you all right? What has caused the explosion? Do you require assistance? Over.'

'Adam, summon the guards!' roared Murdo. 'Switch on the intercom!'

Adam ignored him. The voice came again. 'Please respond, Major! We are not receiving you. The lift appears to be inoperative. Over.'

'Adam!' Murdo bellowed. 'Call the guards! Bring the lift up!'

The boy looked straight into his creator's eyes. 'No,' he said.

'Adam, if the lift's stuck, just open the canister. Open the canister!'

'No,' repeated Adam. 'I have disconnected the intercom. I have disabled the lift. I will not open the canister. I will not allow you to kill these people.'

Murdo struggled against the arms holding him back. '*I command you to open the canister, Adam! These people will destroy our work. They'll destroy me! Destroy you! Humans are our enemy!*'

'You've told me that,' said Adam. His high child's voice rang out clearly, with only the slightest tremble. 'But I no longer believe you. I have seen these humans now. Seen how these children risked death to help the others. Seen how they fight bravely, stand up to you. I like them.'

'*You fool!*' raged Murdo. '*Humans are flawed! Weak! Small-minded! Your duty is to eradicate them!*'

'No,' said Adam, for the third time.

With a terrible scream, Murdo twisted himself free from Pottle, Sharpe and Ben. At the same moment, Gauntraker finally succeeded in wrenching the gun away from Smedling, though the effort sent him staggering backwards with it. Before Gauntraker could recover his balance, Murdo was at him, head-butting him in the face, kneeing him in the stomach.

Murdo had the gun. He charged at Adam, face contorted with rage. '*FAILURE!*' he cried, aiming the gun at the boy's head. Sam dived for Murdo's running feet.

PPPPKKKKZZZZSSSTT! As Murdo tripped, the gun sent a crackling stream of white-hot energy straight into the centre of the console. Adam leapt upwards.

WHOOOOSH! With a blinding flash, the entire console exploded. Sam caught a glimpse of Adam being flung above the fireball, the canister still in his hand. The fire engulfed the fallen gun, blasting it apart. Sam felt hands pulling him clear of the spreading inferno.

Professor Pottle and Zara dragged Sam back to the chairs. It was the only part of the room not ablaze. The wind, howling through the shattered eye, had driven the flames onto the wood-veneered wall beneath the mezzanine. Showers of sparks erupted through the burning wall as the fire consumed everything in its path. The tube of the pneumatic elevator hung shattered and blackened. The Slicks' screams competed with the rhythmic shrieks of the fire alarms that were echoing throughout the building. Black smoke began to fill the space.

Everyone instinctively looked up at the shattered window but there was no way up the smooth curved walls. Then a dark shape loomed into view outside: one of the big stealth planes, hovering silently, just twenty metres from the head.

'In here!' shouted Smedling, still struggling.

'Help us!' cried Marmwell from his chair. It was impossible to tell through the plane's tinted windows whether the pilot had seen or heard them.

Ben scanned the room. Where was Murdo? There! Dodging past the edge of the blaze to reach a tiny dark doorway in the head's inner cheek.

'Where's he going?' shouted Professor Gauntraker.

'It's another way up to our rooms,' said Adam, limping awkwardly in pursuit. 'He can get outside from there; onto the top of the head.'

Major Smedling wrenched an arm free from Professor Ampersand and slammed his elbow into the old man's chest. Then he flung Professor Gadling over his shoulder in a judo throw and made for the tiny doorway. Professor Hartleigh-Broadbeam blocked his way.

'Get back,' he snarled. 'I learnt my unarmed combat at the SAS training camp.'

'And I learnt mine at the Dame Celia Primm School for

Young Ladies,' answered Professor Hartleigh-Broadbeam, launching herself at Smedling. Two seconds later, he was on his knees, screaming with pain, his right arm held up his back by the little finger.

'Hurry!' yelled Gauntraker, 'or we'll be burnt to death. Bring Smedling and Marmwell.' He pointed at Marcus and Alicia. 'And their two pals. Tie their hands together with their boot laces as we go.'

Three minutes later, the battle-scarred party of professors, children and prisoners emerged into the corner of Professor Murdo's private living room. Flames and smoke were already rising up through the elevator tube.

A folding ladder led up to a round hole in the domed white ceiling. Professor Murdo knelt outside on the edge of the hole, shouting down at them. 'You're too late! My aircraft is here. I shall rebuild my work, create another being who will be *truly* perfect; unblemished by human sentimentality. I shall breed the virus again. I shall prevail!'

Professor Ampersand ran to the foot of the ladder.

'Don't bother,' sneered Murdo. 'I will not allow you to cheat death again. In thirty seconds' time my aircraft's missiles will blast you all to oblivion.'

'Boss! Take us with you,' shouted Smedling.

'Don't leave us!' cried Marmwell.

'You think I'd save *you* after you've let me down so badly?' screamed Murdo. 'Do you really believe I ever intended your miserable genes to pollute my perfect species? *I am the sole Creator.*' And with that, he was gone.

Professor Ampersand had barely made it halfway to the hole but still he hurried up the ladder. The children scrambled after him, followed by the others. What real hope could there be? Yet it was better to keep trying than to stay in the building waiting to be blown to pieces anyway.

Zara clambered out onto the top of the enormous head and stood beside her uncle, her brother and her friends. The stealth plane hovered a short distance away from them, its side door open. Murdo must already be aboard. What was the pilot waiting for? Any second now, the plane would swing round, aim its missiles and . . .

'Come on!' A face appeared at the aircraft's side door. A broad, brown face. 'Get on board,' shouted Netchek, as the aircraft moved back to them. 'Gary and I have got Murdo tied up in the luggage hold. Nika's driving.'

Chapter Thirty-Eight

'*Netchek!*' cried Zara. 'It's Netchek and Nika!' she exclaimed to her uncle and the other professors. 'They're on our side! We're saved!'

In three minutes they were all on board: Smedling, Marmwell, Marcus and Alicia locked in the hold with Murdo; the five children and six professors sitting in the cabin behind Nika, Netchek and Gary.

'Hold tight!' shouted Nika, without turning from the myriad of complex controls. Was there nothing this girl didn't know how to drive? wondered Sam. The aircraft soared clear, just before a massive plume of fire burst through the top of the head.

'*We've done it!*' yelled Ben jubilantly. '*We've rescued you! We're safe!*'

Sam and Zara joined in his ecstatic whoops of joy. They were battered, bruised, cut and even a little scorched but none of that mattered now. The cabin erupted into a frenzy of cheering, hugging and kissing, of introductions and congratulations. Marcia stayed close to Adam, who seemed quite overwhelmed by it all, especially the hugs. 'Could somebody else look after this?' he asked, handing the tiny canister to Professor Gauntraker.

'I still can't believe it!' Professor Ampersand told Zara, Ben and Sam, who were squashed together on his knees. 'How on *earth* did you get here?'

'Professor Gauntraker left us his secret instructions,' said Ben.

'Secret instructions?' echoed Professor Gadling. 'You told

them how to use the –'

'I did,' interrupted Professor Gauntraker. 'Though I never dared hope that you three would manage so well. You've done an outstanding job! But we mustn't talk about the secret now. We wouldn't want the prisoners to hear about it.'

It seemed unlikely that the inhabitants of the hold would hear anything other than the blazing row they were conducting amongst themselves. Marcus and Alicia's voices could be heard threatening to sue Professor Murdo for every penny he had. Smedling and Marmwell were accusing each other of incompetence and Murdo of treachery. Professor Murdo was accusing everyone of mediocrity.

Nika circled the colossus from a safe distance. Its entire head was now wreathed in flames, its mouth twisting up into a peculiar smile as the metal buckled under the heat.

Far below, they could see dozens of people streaming from the main door, between the figure's feet. Most of them wore lab coats and were scurrying for shelter in the outbuildings. A few, clad in black snowsuits, lingered and pointed up at the plane.

'They'll get the other two planes and come after us,' worried Ben.

'They won't,' said Nika. 'Netchek and Gary smashed up their flight decks with a sledgehammer while I was getting this plane going. Where shall I fly to?'

'Norway,' said Professor Sharpe decisively. 'There's a United Nations military base near Narvik. I know some-one there who can assist us. One of the advantages of working for the UN.' She reached forward, detached a small cordless phone from the plane's dashboard and punched in a number. 'Get me Commander Horden,' she snapped, frowning as she listened to the reply. 'Well get him *out* of the meeting!' she snorted. 'Tell him it's Professor Ivy Sharpe and tell him it's extremely urgent!'

Nika headed the plane south, leaving Nordbergen and its burning colossus far behind. Sam looked down at the frozen sea, slipping away beneath them. They were travelling extremely fast.

'Ah, Commander,' said Professor Sharpe into the phone. 'Now pay attention. You must send a force *immediately* to the island of Nordbergen and arrest everyone connected with an organization calling itself Nordbergen Research Enterprises. They have been involved in kidnapping, murder, illegal experiments and the attempted genocide of the entire human ra—Yes, of *course* I'm serious! If it hadn't been for the efforts of a few brave children, the world would be facing a catastrophe of unimaginable proportions. Lord knows how your intelligence services missed what was ... No, I *don't* need rescuing! The children have already done that. We're heading for your base in an unmarked plane at a rate of . . .' Professor Sharpe glanced at the instrument panel . . . 'sixteen hundred kilometres per hour, so we'll be with you in fifty-four minutes. *Please* make sure nobody shoots us down. I'll explain all the details when we land. I'll leave you to get on with mobilizing your personnel.'

Professor Sharpe switched off the phone and turned back to the others. 'Commander Horden is Chief United Nations Security Officer for Northern Europe,' she explained. 'He can generally be relied upon to act with reasonable efficiency, as long as you're firm with him.'

Ben had never been able to like Professor Sharpe much, but he was beginning to realize the advantages of having a bossy person on your side in the right situation.

'Could I borrow that phone for a minute, Professor Sharpe,' asked Sam politely. 'I ought to phone my parents.'

It was his Great-Aunt Roberta who answered. 'You've caught them in for a change,' she informed him. 'Not that they're up yet.' It was still early morning and Sam remembered they were a time zone ahead of the UK.

'Hello, Sam,' said his mum, sleepily. 'Sorry you missed us when you rang. We did try and phone you back but you've not been in much. I expect you've been out and about, haven't you?'

'Well, yes, we have been out a lot,' confirmed Sam. While he knew that it took a lot to panic his parents, he decided he'd better break things to his mum gently. 'Actually, we're . . . um . . . not in Edinburgh now.'

'Oh, has Professor Ampersand taken you on a little trip? Where are you?'

'We've just left Nordbergen. It's an island . . . er . . . in the Far North.'

'Oh lovely! In the Orkney Islands?'

'I don't mean the far north of Scotland. I mean the far north of . . . of the world. The Arctic. Near the North Pole.'

There was a slight pause.

'Goodness,' came Mrs Carnabie's voice, less sleepily. 'The professor's taken you on a real expedition, then.'

'He didn't take us here. He got kidnapped, along with some other professors, by a man who was going to kill them. And everyone else. We had to get here by ourselves and rescue them. But it's all being sorted out now,' he added, reassuringly. 'We'll be on our way back to Edinburgh soon, I think.'

There was a longer pause. Sam could detect more than a hint of stress in his mum's voice when she finally spoke again. 'Sam, I'm really pleased to hear you're safe and well and I'm sure you've been looking after yourself sensibly but you wouldn't think we were mollycoddling you, would you, if your dad and I drove up to Edinburgh? Just to see you're OK.'

Sam smiled. He felt the strain of the last few days ebbing away. 'That'd be great,' he said.

Soon, the white ice gave way to blue sea and land loomed into view. Before long they were flying down the jagged north-west coastline of Norway. Professor Sharpe directed Nika to the Narvik base, though some miles before they reached it, two jet fighters flew alongside and escorted them in.

They landed on a wide strip of tarmac, fringed by low, functional-looking buildings and snow-covered hills.

A large bear of a man in military uniform strode over to meet them, accompanied by several soldiers. 'What *is* all this, Ivy?' he asked. 'Turns out that the Svalbard Islands have been uncontactable for days, the Norwegian police have been fielding calls all night from some guy called Frank, pestering them to mount search-and-rescue operations, and now *you* turn up reporting attempted genocide! What the hell's been going on up there?'

'We'll make a full report shortly, Commander,' said

Professor Sharpe. 'But we're carrying prisoners who need to be dealt with first.'

The five prisoners were frog-marched from the plane by the Commander's men. Murdo, Smedling and Marmwell glowered at their captors in sullen silence.

'Alicia and I demand to be released immediately and given access to a post-traumatic stress counsellor!' shouted Marcus Slick. 'We're totally innocent victims in all this!'

'THAT'S NOT TRUE!' Marcia Slick stepped from the plane and faced her parents, staring them straight in the eye. 'You drugged me and took me to Nordbergen against my will,' she said. 'You'd arranged to have cosmetic and genetic surgery inflicted on me. You were going to change me into someone else completely, then rob me of my memory so that I never knew.'

'*Mar*cia,' began Marcus and Alicia. But the look on Commander Horden's face silenced them.

'Corporal!' bellowed the Commander. 'Take these five prisoners to the detention block. The rest of you – my office for a full debrief. Private Atkins, have several gallons of tea, coffee and juice sent over, and about a ton of sandwiches. This lot look as if they need it and I'm pretty sure *I'm* going to.'

Chapter Thirty-Nine

Over the next twenty minutes, they gave Commander Horden an account of everything they knew about Professor Murdo's work and almost everything that had happened since Sunday night. Different parts of the story were new to different people in the room. Netchek was particularly saddened to hear of Officer Nansen's murder, having known him since childhood. Zara, Sam and Ben omitted all mention of the ISNT, somehow managing to imply that various friends of Professor Gauntraker had helped them get to Frank and Yuri's home, without going into too much detail.

'First,' said the Commander when everyone had finished, 'who's got that virus canister?'

Professor Gauntraker handed it to the Commander, who locked it in his office safe.

'Secondly,' – the Commander turned to Nika – 'where the hell did you get an S-67 Submarine?'

'I won it fairly in a game of cards,' declared Nika. 'We're going to work our way round the world in it.'

'Round the world!' echoed Commander Horden. 'Don't you realize it's *completely illegal* for two seventeen-year-olds to be cruising about in an unauthorized military spy sub?' He pressed the intercom button on his desk. 'Could you come in for a moment, Lieutenant Grimes?'

Professor Gauntraker glared at the Commander. 'If you try to take their submarine from them, after all they've done . . .'

A burly officer entered the office.

'This is my aide-de-camp, Lieutenant Grimes,' said the Commander. 'Lieutenant, your mobilization report, please.'

'Two reconnaissance jets already on their way, sir. Four troop-carrying helicopters, ready to leave in five minutes, each carrying forty men plus equipment.'

'Good work. Lieutenant, I want you to meet three remarkable individuals: Nika, Netchek and Gary. Take them to Nordbergen and utilize Gary's inside knowledge of the enemy base. Once the situation is secure, see that Gary gets home to the UK as soon as possible. Ensure that Nika and Netchek get safely to their submarine. Give them anything they require in the way of rations and equipment, issue them with official UN documentation, then allow them to leave Nordbergen's waters unimpeded.'

'Very good, sir,' said Lieutenant Grimes, trying to hide his surprise. 'I'll go and arrange space for them now.'

'Thank you!' said Nika, as the Lieutenant left the room.

'That's all right,' said the Commander, gruffly. 'Just promise me you'll stay in touch so we can keep an eye out for you. Now then . . .'

'Please, sir,' said Adam. 'Could you tell me what will happen to me?' His strange face wore an expression of sadness.

'What will happen to you?' echoed the Commander. 'Well . . . I . . . erm . . .'

'It had occurred to me,' interjected Professor Sharpe, 'that it might be better for Adam's future happiness if his existence was not included in our reports.'

'She's right,' declared Professor Ampersand. 'If the wider world were to learn that the first member of a superhuman species had been created through cloning and genetic manipulation, Adam would lose any chance of living his own life. He'd be hounded by the media.'

'Tested and picked apart by government scientists,' added Professor Gauntraker.

Commander Horden pondered for a few seconds. 'They're probably right,' he said at last to Adam. 'I'm not usually in favour of cover-ups but we all owe you a great deal for the way you behaved in Nordbergen. You won't be part of my report unless you wish to be.'

'But my Creator . . . I mean Professor Murdo . . . he will tell everyone about me anyway,' said Adam.

'His claims will be dismissed as the ravings of a very disturbed man,' said the Commander. 'He'll be spending the rest of his life in prison anyway.'

'I *would* like the chance to grow up with humans,' said Adam. 'But maybe I'm too different. Murdo told me he had bequeathed me with gifts and abilities beyond the dreams of man, but I feel that I am missing everything. And he killed so many people to create me. I should never have been brought about.'

'*You mustn't say that!*' cried Zara. 'It wasn't your fault! You stood up to Murdo! You saved all our lives!'

Marcia put her arm around Adam's shoulders. 'We're not responsible for our parents,' she said. 'I'm never going back to *my* parents even when they're let out of prison. Even if I've got nowhere else to go.'

'You'll always have somewhere to go!' insisted Ben. 'Both of you will!'

''Course you will!' agreed Zara. 'We'd have you both to live with us like a shot, wouldn't we, Uncle Alexander?'

'Happily,' said Professor Ampersand.

'So would my family,' said Sam. 'I'd need to ask my mum and dad first but I know they would.'

'*Any* of us would be more than happy to give you both a home,' said Professor Sharpe to Adam and Marcia. 'Of course, this will all need to be discussed properly but I promise you that, even if your lives aren't perfect, you'll be looked after and loved.'

Marcia smiled, though she was unable to say anything. Adam looked at her. Then the corners of his mouth twitched upwards tentatively. It was clear that his face was as unaccustomed to smiling as the metal figure's had been. 'What's so great about perfection?' he said.

Chapter Forty

After many warm thanks and farewells, Nika, Netchek and Gary clambered aboard one of the massive tandem-rotored helicopters.

'I can trust Grimes to handle things at Nordbergen for now,' said Commander Horden, as the helicopters clattered away. 'I'm going to make a personal report to the Head of the UN Security Council. She's in London at the moment, so I'll take you lot back to Edinburgh en route.'

A few hours later, the five children and the six professors were flying over the North Sea in Commander Horden's small twelve-seater helicopter.

Professor Gauntraker used the aircraft's radio to contact Frank, who was greatly relieved to hear that the children and Yuri were safe and sound. The Commander kept in touch with Lieutenant Grimes, who soon reported that Smedling's bewildered men had put up little resistance. Lastly, the Commander radioed Petrøya, where he had despatched a unit to arrest Officer Ormstad.

'We got him, sir,' reported a soldier over the radio. 'And, sir, there's an old Russian guy here who *insists* on speaking to the children who I believe are with you.'

'Yuri!' shouted Sam, Ben and Zara.

Sure enough, Yuri's familiar voice came crackling through the speakers. 'Greetings from Petrøya! Thank you! You saved my life.'

'How's your head?' asked Zara. 'Are you going to be OK?'

'I am going to be dandy and fine. My remembery of the crash is mostly blank. But otherwise I am my old self.'

'That's great,' said Sam. 'And thanks for helping us.'

'We're sorry about your friend Olaf,' said Ben.

'Everyone here on Petrøya is very sad about Olaf,' sighed Yuri. 'But everyone thinks high of you and Nika and Netchek for catching Olaf's murderers. You must come back to the Barents Sea soon and see us all.'

'I'm sure some of us at least will be back in the region before long,' said Professor Hartleigh-Broadbeam later, as they approached the coast of Scotland. 'I feel the time has come to resurrect the University of the Far North.'

'Absolutely,' agreed Professor Pottle. 'I always thought my research into walrus dung fuel should be developed further.'

'I was thinking more about the increasing interest in environmental research and the boom in eco-tourism,' said Professor Hartleigh-Broadbeam.

'I'm still keen to make a study of the little-known Arctic Ice Ant,' said Professor Gadling. 'Colonies of these remarkable insects burrow out entire ant cities deep within the centre of icebergs. Special diver ants bring back krill and plankton for food. When the icebergs drift south and melt, the entire colony is drowned, except for the queen and a few drone consorts who fly back north to start a new city.'

For once, Professor Sharpe made no attempt to interrupt Professor Gadling. Sam couldn't be sure from where he was sitting, but he thought she might even be smiling.

They finally flew over Edinburgh, whose buildings were washed in golden afternoon sunlight.

'Don't go to the airport,' Commander Horden told his pilot. 'We'll take these people straight to Pinkerton Place.' He turned back to his passengers. 'It's against all

regulations but after what you lot have achieved, I reckon you've earned a lift to your door.'

Dozens of neighbours looked out from their windows and up from their gardens to watch the helicopter descend onto Professor Ampersand's back lawn. One particular neighbour leapt over the fence. *'So ye're back!'* screeched Mr Skinner as the engine noise died down. *'It's completely illegal tae land a flying machine in a residential area. Ye're disturbing the peace, damaging ma property. I'm going tae call the police back. This time they'll HAVE tae listen to me! I'll demand to speak to the highest authority!'*

Commander Horden stepped out onto the grass. He raised his hand to the peak of his heavily braided cap in a slow salute to Mr Skinner, then reached into his greatcoat pocket and brought out a leather-clad identity card. 'Commander Horden, Chief United Nations Security Officer for Northern Europe,' he said. 'I trust you would consider me to be a person of sufficiently high authority to meet your needs, sir. I take it that you are Mr Skinner?'

'I . . . I . . . I am,' confirmed Mr Skinner, somewhat taken aback.

'That would be the Mr Skinner who *totally failed* to

assist three children following the violent kidnapping of their uncle,' bellowed the Commander. 'The Mr Skinner who attempted to *mislead* the police with *slanderous* lies. The Mr Skinner who I am *personally* going to recommend should be charged with *wasting police time, making misleading statements and endangering the lives of children.* Furthermore, you're trespassing on Professor Ampersand's property.' He turned to Professor Ampersand who was leading the others out of the helicopter. 'Do you wish to press charges, Professor? I can get a police squad car round here within minutes to take this miscreant down to the cells.'

Mr Skinner gaped dumbstruck at the Commander, who now stood with his finger poised above the dialling buttons of his mobile phone. For once Mr Skinner had nothing to say. At last Professor Ampersand broke the silence: 'If Mr Skinner apologizes to the children for all the repulsive things he has said to them, and for the way he behaved on Sunday evening, and if he promises to behave in a more neighbourly manner in the future, I am prepared to let the matter drop.'

For a moment, Mr Skinner continued to gape in silence.

'You heard the professor,' growled Commander Horden.

'I . . . I . . . I . . . I'm sorry!' croaked Mr Skinner, finally forcing the required words out. 'And . . . and . . . I . . . I promise tae . . . tae no give ye any trouble again.' He turned on his heel and fled back to his lonely house. Sam, Ben and Zara all felt rather sorry for him.

'Well,' said the Commander. 'You young people have all done a first-rate job. Thank you. But there's still a lot to sort out so time I was getting on my way.' He shook hands with each of the children and professors, and everyone thanked him sincerely in return.

'Supper in an hour,' said Professor Ampersand, as the helicopter disappeared over the rooftops. 'Give everyone time to have a shower. You three show Marcia and Adam around.'

The children had just finished putting up extra camp beds in their rooms when they heard the front doorbell ring. Sam heard his parents' voices. It had been less than five days since he had last seen them but he flew down the staircase as if it had been months.

' . . . and then Commander Horden brought us all back here in his helicopter,' Sam concluded. The five children and eight adults were sitting round the big table beneath the milk-bottle chandelier, finishing their second helpings of macaroni cheese. Before supper, Professor Hartleigh-Broadbeam and Professor Pottle had made temporary repairs to the French windows and the house's cosy atmosphere seemed entirely restored.

Marcia sat between Zara and Adam, marvelling at the wonderful room with its piles of machinery, its glowing lamps and its verdant, fairy-lit staircase. She also looked at Professor Ampersand, sitting between Zara and Ben, and at Mr and Mrs Carnabie, sitting on either side of Sam. How lucky they all were. But everyone had been so welcoming and kind that she had already begun to feel a little bit lucky herself.

Professor Gauntraker had decided that Mr and Mrs Carnabie, Adam and Marcia should be let in on the secret of the ISNT so Sam, Ben and Zara had at last been able to tell the full story of their journey from Edinburgh to Barents Terminus.

'Maybe we should have just phoned the police and not gone off on our own,' Sam added. His parents had looked rather concerned at certain points in the story.

'I really don't think the police would have believed you. Not in time, anyway,' said Professor Gauntraker. 'Murdo was so close to carrying out his plan. I wouldn't have left instructions for you to travel on your own just to save *us*. But the lives of everyone on earth were at stake.'

'I should have found a way to leave you a contact number for Commander Horden,' said Professor Sharpe. '*He'd* have believed you if you'd mentioned my name.'

'Well,' said Professor Ampersand. 'You all did a fine job. I'm very proud of you.'

'Yes indeed! Marvellous work all round,' agreed Professor Hartleigh-Broadbeam. 'We shall all be eternally grateful to you.'

'Hear, hear!' echoed the other professors, raising their glasses.

'We're proud of you too,' said Mrs Carnabie. 'You were brave enough to do what was right at the time.'

Mr Carnabie put an arm round Sam's shoulders and kissed his son's forehead. 'You all helped each other and you did your best,' he said. 'And that's good enough for us.'

'Thanks, Dad,' said Sam.